CARNIVAL

➤➤ of the ☜

LOST

FABER has published children's books since 1929. T. S. Eliot's *Old Possum's Book of Practical Cats* and Ted Hughes' *The Iron Man* were among the first. Our catalogue at the time said that 'it is by reading such books that children learn the difference between the shoddy and the genuine'. We still believe in the power of reading to transform children's lives. All our books are chosen with the express intention of growing a love of reading, a thirst for knowledge and to cultivate empathy. We pride ourselves on responsible editing. Last but not least, we believe in kind and inclusive books in which all children feel represented and important.

KIERAN LARWOOD is the award-winning and bestselling author of the Five Realms series that started with *The Legend of Podkin One-Ear*. He was a teacher but now writes full-time although, if anybody was watching, they might think he just daydreams a lot.

SAM USHER is a multi-award-winning illustrator. His books include the Seasons series, *The Birthday Duck*, *The Most-Loved Bear* and *The Umbrella Mouse*. Also a talented pianist, when he's not scribbling you'll find him perfecting a fiendishly difficult Chopin piece.

THE CARNIVAL OF THE LOST SERIES

Carnival of the Lost

THE FIVE REALMS SERIES

The Legend of Podkin One-Ear
The Gift of Dark Hollow
The Beasts of Grimheart

Uki and the Outcasts
Uki and the Swamp Spirit
Uki and the Ghostburrow

CARNIVAL of the LOST

LOST

KIERAN LARWOOD

Illustrated by Sam Usher

faber

First published in 2022
by Faber & Faber Limited
Bloomsbury House,
74–77 Great Russell Street,
London WC1B 3DA
faberchildrens.co.uk

Typeset in Times New Roman by Faber
Printed by CPI Group (UK) Ltd,
Croydon CR0 4YY

A CIP record for this book is available from the British Library

ISBN 978–0–571–36450–3

FSC
www.fsc.org
MIX
Paper from
responsible sources
FSC® C171272

2 4 6 8 10 9 7 5 3

Prologue

Midnight.

The heart-of-summer sky was black; filled with stars, the cloudy sweep of the Milky Way. A waxing moon slowly rolled across, showing off her pockmarks and craters, looking down at a smaller, man-made galaxy: the gas and oil lamps, candles and lanterns of old London town, twinkling their brightest and – through a haze of smog – bravely trying to outdo the heavens themselves.

Each window seemed to be ablaze, every church steeple and cobblestone bathed in light. The centre of the city was wide awake, even at this late hour.

Horses clopped up and down Oxford Street and

around Covent Garden. Crowds of well-dressed gentlefolk strolled from inn to opera house, filling the air with the sound of chatter and laughter. Diamond necklaces glinted, gilded walking canes tapped. Baronets and ladies bowed and curtsied.

This was the London that history books remembered. These were the scenes painters hung on the walls of museums and art galleries.

But there was another side to the city entirely. A true side. A dark side.

It didn't have all the lights and glamour. It didn't sparkle and shine like midnight constellations. Grubby and cruel, it hid down fog-choked alleys and inside crumbling houses. Soot-smeared and spiteful, it hoarded its secrets under a blanket of smoke and cinders.

It didn't want to be seen, but you couldn't avoid the smell. The stink. The unholy, nose-melting *stench*.

The River Thames gave it away. As it ran through the heart of crowded London – threading together palaces, towers, factories, docks and slums alike – it slowly filled with the most awful soup of ingredients.

Rotting things. Dead things. Cast-away, spewed-up, flushed-out . . . *stuff.*

It had an aroma like nothing on earth, tenderly brewed in its waters and wafted, with loving care, up among the narrow streets, where it was trapped by the thick shroud of dust and mist that covered the city.

The place boiled with bad air. It seethed with stink, pulsed with pong.

And down by the river itself it was worst of all. You could almost carve slices out of the air with a bread knife.

It was the ripest, most putrid place in the whole of London. Nobody with a working nose went near it, unless they had a really good reason, which made it perfect for meetings of the shady, secret kind.

One of which was happening right now.

*

Three figures stood on the shoreline, boots crunching on the thin strip of pebbles and broken glass that ran along the edge of the bank, like a dirty mark around a bathtub.[i]

Broken, weed-covered ribs of wrecked boats jutted up from the mud around them. On the banks above, warehouses loomed, locked up and silent. The occasional watchman wandered between them, bullseye lantern gleaming in the dark.

'Is it finished?' one of the figures asked. He was smaller than the other two, stooped, with frizzy hair that poked from either side of a bald head.

'Yes, it is,' said another. The shadowy outline of her flowing skirts and corset caught the moonlight as she reached out to pat a covered mound next to her on the bank. A soft clang sounded and was quickly swallowed by the mist. 'Did you bring the . . . specimens?'

'We did,' said the stooped man. He motioned to the third figure, who lifted up a hefty sack, dropping it to the ground between them. As it landed, something pale and spidery flopped from the opening. A small hand with thin, bony fingers. Bloodless. Dead.

The second speaker jumped in shock, then laughed at herself. She bent to inspect the sack's contents, rummaging around in the dark. 'For a second,' she said, her voice muffled by the hessian, 'I thought that was a dead person. Looks very similar, does it not?'

'I have a theory about that . . .' the stooped man began, but the third figure silenced him with a growl.

'Will they suffice?' he asked. 'That's all I need to know.' His voice was deep, stern. Someone you would think twice about disobeying.

The silhouette of the woman stood. Nodded. 'They've been dead quite a while, but they'll do.'

'Then our business is done,' said the third figure. 'As long as it works.'

'Oh, it does,' said the woman. 'You can test it if you like . . .'

A curtain of mist billowed past, hiding the three shadows from sight. Strange, unearthly sounds began to echo along the riverbank. Hisses, clicks, crunches. A muffled, metallic roar and then, with a wet slithering and the ripple of filthy water, something alien slid down into the mud and vanished beneath the surface . . .

CHAPTER ONE

In which our heroine's life takes a dramatic turn.

Sheba gazed through her tiny window at the pier's end, to the seaside view beyond. It was a beautiful summer morning. The sounds of the beach drifted in and she closed her eyes to hear them better. Children splashing and laughing. The cries of gulls. She smelled the tang of fresh seaweed, tasted salt on the breeze. Her mind drifted, down to the sand and pebbles below. She could almost feel the waves lapping around her toes and the sun toasting her face.

Almost thought she could turn and race along the beach, leaving a trail of footprints behind her.

But such things were not meant for her, and dreaming about them only made it worse. Sheba gave a deep sigh and began running her comb through her chestnut-brown curls, taking out the tangles. She always took great care of her locks. Everyone said she had a lovely head of hair.

And face of hair. And hands of hair.

In fact, Sheba was covered in it, from head to foot.

It wasn't all the same hair, of course. Her face and body had a fine, fair coating that might be mistaken for tanned skin, from a distance. She could even have passed for normal in a crowd, if it wasn't for her other unusual features.

Her eyes were a deep amber colour; in a certain light they seemed to have an orange glow. She had small, sharp white teeth and her hands were tipped with nails that looked more than a little like claws. But – far stranger than that – there was a wild wolf sharing her body and when she lost control (or if she let it) more and more of it would slip free.

Her nose stretched into a snout, bristling with

fangs and fur. Her eyes gleamed with an ancient, deadly hunger. She was then filled with the urge to run on all fours, howling, snapping and growling.

Anyone who saw it – especially if they were on the snarling end – soon started calling her 'Sheba the Wolfgirl'. A name she hated beyond all hatred.

And worse, they began to avoid her, as if she were some kind of wild animal. The whispers spread, the stares became filled with fear. It made her feel like a monster. A creature from a penny horror book. It was all so unfair.

If they had just bothered to get to know her, they would have discovered that, although the hair and teeth were the *first* things they noticed, they weren't the most interesting. Sheba was actually an exceptional eight-year-old girl. Her sense of smell was amazing: she could follow a trail like a bloodhound and read scents like the pages of a book. She had a sixth sense: mechanical things seemed to speak to her . . . Any locks she came across popped themselves open with just a few wiggles of her hairpins. And, by the age of five, she had taught herself to read from scraps of newspaper and chalk billboards. She would have liked to read a novel or two, but it was quite difficult to wander into the local library when you were locked in a cage at a seaside curiosity show. And that was where she had spent every minute of every long day for as long as she could remember.

Grunchgirdle's World of Wonders perched at the end of the rickety Little Pilchton pier, like a jackdaw on a branch. Mr Grunchgirdle, the owner, was a skinny old man who smelled of rotten kippers. Besides Sheba, the other attractions were a stuffed squirrel with a carp's tail sewn where its legs should be ('the world's only true mermaid!'[ii]) and a two-headed lamb called Flossy. They all lived crammed into a one-roomed shack no bigger than a large cupboard and were forbidden to ever leave.

It was a poor place to call home, and Sheba spent many hours wondering how she had ended up in it. There had been an orphanage before. A dark, miserable place that Grunchgirdle had bought her from. But earlier than that . . . surely there must have been a mother? A father? Sometimes, when he was feeling particularly cruel, her owner told her that her parents had died of shock when Sheba was born.

Sometimes, she believed him.

But there were hints of memories; wispy threads that came to her in the secret moments before waking. *A large house. Cool marble floor beneath her bare feet. Scorched blue skies outside.*

These things always faded as her eyes opened, crumbling into fragments of dreams and wishes.

When Sheba had finished grooming, she carefully put her comb inside the ebony box that held all her belongings: hairpins, some crumpled pamphlets and a sea-worn limpet shell someone had once dropped on the sideshow floor. As for the box itself, Sheba had no idea where it had come from, only that it had always been hers. She remembered clutching it with terrified claws, the day she was dragged from the orphanage. Which meant it must have been from her previous life. Had it belonged to her mother, perhaps? Or was it a gift from a loving relative? Many nights she lay awake, tracing the carved flowers on its lid with her fingers and wondering. Delicate flowers, with five narrow petals, like stars.

Flossy raised one of his heads from the sorry pile of straw he lay on and gave a weak bleat. Sheba didn't think he appeared to be in the best of health, but that was hardly surprising. Lambs were meant to be out frolicking and gambolling, not waiting in a dim shack for customers that never appeared. If he didn't get some fresh air soon, he wouldn't be long for this world.

Grunchgirdle had spent the last of his money on Flossy a year ago in an attempt to make his tatty sideshow famous. But no one visited Little Pilchton any more. People travelled to places that had railway stations or fast coach routes. The tiny town barely had a road, only a collection of massive potholes linked together by smaller potholes. Grunchgirdle could have bought a seven-headed purple tiger and been no better off.

Sheba offered Flossy a handful of oats, but he just sniffed at them and gave her a dismal look. She patted one of his heads, thinking how sorry she would be if he died. He was the closest thing she had to company. Grunchgirdle treated Sheba no better than an animal. Customers – whenever they turned up – just stood and gawked at her as she sat in her gloomy cage. Unless she summoned up her wolfish side. *Then* they ran out of the shack screaming, while Sheba snapped her teeth at the bars and howled.

What would become of them if Grunchgirdle finally sold up? Poor Flossy would probably end up as a plate of lamb chops, and the squirrel-mermaid would get flung back in the sea, but who would want anything to do with a hairy wolfgirl?

Leaving the oats in a corner of his cage in case Flossy changed one – or both – of his minds, Sheba rummaged in the straw until she found her latest treasure: a five-week-old copy of the *London Examiner*, scavenged from a bin. Hiding it in Flossy's straw was a gamble. If Grunchgirdle found it he would be furious; firstly, to find out Sheba could actually read, and secondly, to discover she had been outside, ferreting through rubbish, when he was asleep. But she never strayed more than five or six yards from the shack on her nocturnal expeditions. [iii] Any further and she might not have been able to get back inside in time if she heard Grunchgirdle stirring in his sleep, and then she would be in for a beating and a half.

Feeling the splinters of the pier under her feet, the

salty wind all around her and the endless swell of the sea beneath the planks was enough. Those same waves broke on shores far away from Little Pilchton. Places she might be lucky enough to see for herself one day . . .

Sheba flicked to the last thing she had been reading, an article about the Great Exhibition of the Industry of All Nations.[iv] As far as she could make out between the old coffee stains, it was a magical collection of the most original and incredible creations of man, gathered together in London, in a fairytale palace made of crystal. There were giant diamonds, stuffed elephants, machines that tipped you out of bed, pictures made of hair (she found that particularly intriguing), knives with thousands of blades, some revolutionary new engine for creating 'electrical impulses' (whatever they were) and machines that did everything from making envelopes to harvesting crops. If it hadn't been written in a newspaper, she wouldn't have believed it.

She wasn't sure she actually *did* believe it. With a snort she flipped the page and was about to start on an article about Prince Albert's favourite trousers, when she caught an overpowering whiff of stale smoke and sweat. It was a few hundred yards away, but getting steadily stronger. Someone was walking up the pier. Surely not a customer? On the off-chance that it might be, she hid the paper, climbed into her cage and quickly locked it shut with one of her hairpins. She sat on her stool and arranged her threadbare dress as neatly as possible, ready to be gawped at.

Then she went to that door in her head: the secret room, the place where the wolf lived. Inching it open, she let part of the beast out. Just a sliver, an inkling. Enough to show the hint of a muzzle, the tips of fangs and curve of claws. But always, always keeping the snarls, howls and bites in check.

Usually she tried to empty her mind as well – so she didn't have to bear the stares, screams and insults – but this time she couldn't help wondering what was going on outside.

The smoky, sweaty scent of the stranger was getting stronger. And now there were heavy footprints on the warped planks of the pier. She could smell Grunchgirdle, too. The bony old goat would be sitting on his milking stool by the pier railing, his fishing line cast out, waiting for supper – or a customer – to come by.

Sure enough, there came the squeak of his stool as the measly old miser sat bolt upright. *He's seen his prey*, Sheba thought. She could imagine his scrawny heart thudding away in his chest. Maybe a bead of sweat forming on his pasty brow, or even a drop of dribble escaping from his thin lips as he thought about what the penny admission fee would get him for dinner. A carrot, or perhaps even a potato to go with the usual fishy broth.

The stranger probably only wanted a bit of fresh air and a stroll down the pier. But he'd soon end up staring at a hairy girl, a wilted lamb and a bad example of fish-based taxidermy.

The footsteps came to a sudden halt. There was a clatter as Grunchgirdle leaped to his feet, knocking his rod and bucket over.

'Good morning, fine sir,' came his reedy voice. 'And how may I help you this lovely summer's day?'

When the stranger spoke, his voice was deep and bitter – as if it had been pickled for many years in a brine of misery and spite – but the words were important ones. They would change Sheba's life for ever.

'I've come about the freaks,' he said.

*

The stranger was a big man, tall and wide. His nose was bulbous and scarlet, and a wild tangle of hair stuck out all around the edges of his stovepipe hat. He was wearing a scowl that could have curdled milk.

Sheba found it difficult not to stare back at him. She focused on her feet instead and kept her ears open – at the same time trying to keep her features as wolfish as possible.

'Well, she's not bad, I s'pose, but I've seen hairier,' said the big man. 'That squirrel-fish is a load of tosh, though, and the sheep's nearly dead.'

'Sheba is a real find, Mr Plumpscuttle! And I assure you the lamb is merely resting. He tires so easily, what with all the extra thinking he has to do. When he's refreshed he hops and jumps about like a March hare, so he does!'

'You can't fool me, Grunchgirdle. I've been in the carnival business since afore I could walk, and I know a sick two-headed sheep when I see one. That thing's got a month left at best before it's lying on a dish, smothered in mint sauce.'

Grunchgirdle fawned and whined at the big man for a few minutes more, but Sheba could see from the corner of her eye that his face was set like stone. It looked like a bargain was about to be struck. Was she finally leaving Little Pilchton pier?

The very thought made her heart skip a beat. What kind of a man was this Plumpscuttle? She presumed he must run a sideshow of his own and, judging by the cut of his frock coat, it must be *much* more successful than Grunchgirdle's.

Beneath the whiff of stale gravy and sweat, she could pick up hints of gas, grime and coal dust. London, she thought. Maybe Birmingham or Manchester. What would his show be like? Her head raced with a thousand questions, hopes and fears. She began to feel quite faint.

'Twelve pounds for the girl and the sheep, and that's my final offer,' said Plumpscuttle. 'As for the mermaid, you can stick that where the sun don't shine.'

He pulled a cloth purse from his waistcoat and dangled it before Grunchgirdle's eyes. The scrawny man stared at it, his face torn with indecision. Finally, with a great sigh, he dropped his head and reached for the money.

*

Minutes later, Sheba was walking down the pier beside Mr Plumpscuttle, clutching her ebony box tightly. It held everything she owned in the world besides the clothes on her back. A weak bleat came from the basket Plumpscuttle carried – Sheba was glad Flossy was coming too.

She could hardly believe it: out in the open air, in full daylight, for the first time in years. Her little furry head was reeling. Wide eyes peeped out from the deep hood of her riding cloak. The urge to leap about screaming with joy nearly overtook her, but she got the impression her new owner wouldn't approve.

It felt as if she were walking inside a dream.

The sunlight seemed impossibly bright. It gleamed off the waves, the sand, the hundreds of flapping pennants that hung along the pier. Everything was so vivid it hurt her eyes just to look. And there were such smells. Baking bread and ice cream. Sugared sweets and fresh fish. Ale from the pubs. Hundreds of people: old and young, sick, perfumed, unwashed. She'd never imagined there could be such variety. In between all these were scents she had no name for. Endless new odours rushed up her nose, making her dizzy with the desire to run and chase them to their source.

As they came to the end of the pier, Sheba realised that, when she stepped from the last salt-streaked plank, she would actually be setting foot on solid land again. She wanted to pause and savour the moment, but Plumpscuttle was already striding ahead. She jogged to keep up, enjoying the satisfying thump her feet made on the stone cobbles.

She had imagined Little Pilchton as some kind of exotic world, picturing shop fronts overflowing with silks and spices, great boulevards where grand ladies and gentlemen strolled in their finery, mansions and hotels in elegantly carved stone. Instead it was a dingy old place with a couple of ramshackle pubs and far too many fishmongers. The fantasy world she had yearned to walk in for so long was, like most daydreams, more than a little disappointing.

They soon left the town and crested the brow of a hill. A whole tapestry of fields and woods opened up before them, as wide as the sea and every shade of green. Sheba paused to wonder at the sheer amount of space, and then they were over and down the other side. A narrow dirt track wandered along between hedges and mossy stone walls, and they headed down it, kicking up a cloud of dust behind them.

They walked and walked and walked. It seemed as if they were never going to stop. At last, when Sheba's legs throbbed from top to bottom, her cape was coated in grit from the road and the sun had painted the sky pink, they stumbled to the top of yet another rise.

'We're here,' said Plumpscuttle, the first words he had spoken to her, and he marched through an open five-bar gate into a field. Sheba followed after him, wide eyes taking in everything around her.

There were signs of recent festivities. Colourful bunting was draped along the drystone wall, the grass had been churned by hordes of booted feet, and there were paper wrappers, apple cores and pie crusts everywhere. Show-folk were packing up stalls and rides, and hitching them to horses, before rolling out onto the road and off to the next village fair. Sheba saw a coconut shy, a group of fortune-tellers and a rickety old merry-go-round. The place was a hive of activity, even though the festivities were now over.

Plumpscuttle strode on, nodding to an acquaintance here and there, until they reached the corner of the field. Here stood a canary-yellow caravan, with a towering grey shire horse dozing between the shafts. Painted on the side were dramatic pictures: a giant lifting an elephant above his head; the black silhouette of a long-haired girl, her insides dotted with stars and a crescent moon; a hideous imp stirring a cauldron that spewed purple smoke. And dancing between their legs were little rats, all wearing human clothes.

Sheba's heart began to pound. This was much more exciting than Grunchgirdle's dreary little display: this was a *proper* carnival show.

Plumpscuttle interrupted her thoughts. 'Get in,' he said as he chucked Flossy's basket up onto the driver's seat and heaved himself up beside it. Behind him was a door into the caravan. He kicked it open with a hobnail boot and then, when Sheba had climbed close enough, shoved her through. The door slammed shut after her.

The inside was dark and musty. She could smell people – at least three or four. A match was struck, a lantern lit.

In the candlelight, a cluster of faces appeared, all staring at her intently. They were odd forms, hulking and mismatched. Like nothing she had seen before.

Sheba started to scream.

CHAPTER TWO

In which Sheba experiences the scents of Victorian industry: coal dust, grinding engines and scalding steam.

Once her shrieks had finished, the rhythmic clop of horses' hooves and the gentle sway of the caravan began to soothe Sheba's nerves. Enough, even, for her to brave a quick look around. Plumpscuttle had shoved her into what she now realised was a cosy wooden room on wheels, with a window, shelves, pictures on the walls and even a miniature stove. If it wasn't for the other inhabitants, it would feel like a snug little home.

There were two low bunks on either side, and she

edged forward to sit on one – sneaking glances at her new comrades.

The bulk of a giant, the biggest man she had ever seen, took up almost half the caravan space. He had a shaved head, a craggy face scratched with criss-cross patterns of old scars, and a broad-striped woollen jersey that looked as though it would pop its seams at any second. Squished into a curled ball, he was trying to jot notes in a leather-bound journal, his meaty fingers making the pencil look like a toothpick.

Sitting on the bunk beside Sheba was a slightly older girl dressed in a boy's charcoal-grey suit and trousers. She wore a top hat from which a cascade of ebony-black hair flowed, all the way down to her waist. Spectacles with smoked-glass lenses covered her eyes, making Sheba wonder what she had to hide.

The bunk opposite was occupied by a mysterious figure puffing on a long clay pipe, its face hidden beneath the wide brim of a felt hat. It was only when the person looked up, showing vivid green eyes and soft, greying curls, that Sheba realised it was a woman. She was wearing a patched greatcoat, breeches and knee-high leather boots, and her left arm was resting on a large wooden box, from which Sheba could hear a quiet rustling. It smelled as though some kind of animals were inside, and when the woman caught Sheba staring at it, she gave her a quick wink.

Stranger still, hanging from the roof was a small iron cage and in it was a young boy. His arms dangled through the open door, stretching far longer than a child's arms were supposed to. They poked from his shirt sleeves, covered with bristly grey hair that spread down to his broad, spidery hands, even spilling onto the knobbled joints of his fingers. Fingers that were topped off with curved claws.

The skin of his face was leathery and crinkled, like an old boot left too long in the sun. Wide yellow eyes glared out from under a mop of shaggy hair, and crooked fangs jutted up from his bottom lip.

It was a bizarre set of travelling companions but one in which Sheba the Wolfgirl fitted quite well. She began to feel ashamed about her first reaction.

'I'm sorry I screamed when I saw you,' she said in a quiet voice.

'That's quite all right,' said the woman with the clay pipe, smiling.

'We're used to it,' added the giant, not looking up from his journal.

'Bit of a cheek, though, when you look like an accident in a wig factory,' said the boy.

'Ignore him,' said the woman. 'He's awful rude to everyone he meets, so you mustn't take it personally.'

'It's fine. I don't mind,' said Sheba, although actually she did. 'I am a bit strange, I suppose.'

'As are we all, dearie.' The woman turned to face the room. 'And now you've pulled yourself together, I suppose it's time you were introduced to the company.' She leant forward, and with the end of her pipe, began pointing out the others in the caravan.

'That great mound of might and muscle is known as Gigantus, the man mountain. Strong as a bull, but soft as a duckling on the inside. The young lady beside you is the famous Sister Moon: daughter of the dark but faster than the light. The long-armed creature in the cage is Pyewacket. One of the witch's imps discovered by Matthew Hopkins himself, a full two hundred years ago.'[vi]

As their names were mentioned, they each gave Sheba a glance or a nod. Sheba smiled back, then turned to the woman.

'You didn't tell me *your* name,' she said.

'I didn't? How rude! I am Mama Rat and these here are my little darlings, the cleverest ratties in the country.' She tapped the box beside her, at which a series of squeaks and squeals emerged. 'Hush now,' Mama Rat whispered into one of the holes on the top. 'You can get a good look at her when we stop. Nosy things.' She gave Sheba another wink and blew a few smoke rings from her pipe.

Through the air holes cut into the bottom of the box, Sheba glimpsed the twinkle of cunning little eyes. By instinct, she hated rodents. The ratty stench made her hackles rise. But she managed not to growl. 'My name is Sheba,' she said instead. 'Very pleased to meet you all.' The rats all squeaked excitedly and raced around the edges of their box.

'Did you come from another sideshow?' asked Sister Moon.

'Yes. Grunchgirdle's. At the end of the pier in Little Pilchton.'

'Little *what*?' said Pyewacket.

'We're from London,' explained Mama Rat. 'The East End. Plumpscuttle takes his show on the road for a few weeks each summer, touring the local fairs. That was our last one for the season, so now we're headed home.'

'Just in time,' said Pyewacket. 'My spirit guide told me there's going to be a terrible storm in the countryside. And a plague of giant turnips.'

Gigantus snorted a laugh. 'Are you sure he didn't say "termites"?'

'Ah, yes,' Pyewacket grimaced. 'That's what I meant to say.'

'I've never been to London,' said Sheba. She tingled with excitement at the thought.

'It's stinky, smoky and horrid,' said Sister Moon.

'It's fascinating, fun and beautiful,' said Mama Rat.

'It's a festering cesspit of horror,' said Gigantus, still not bothering to look up from his journal.

Sheba was starting to feel anxious. 'Is Mr Plumpscuttle a nice boss?' she asked, looking to change the subject.

There was a mixture of snorts, coughs and

splutters from around the caravan.

'That depends on whether you like being insulted, spat at, half starved and paraded in front of slack-jawed dimwits night after night. If the answer is yes, then he's the greatest boss in the world,' said Pyewacket with a scowl.

'He's a spiteful swindler,' said Gigantus.

'He smells almost bad as Pyewacket,' said Sister Moon, with a wink.

'Do you mind?' The boy waved his arms and gnashed his teeth, making his cage swing round and round. 'You all know that I'll lose my powers if I wash!'

Sheba wished she had never asked. Perhaps she would have been better off staying with fishy old Grunchgirdle . . .

'Oh, hush yourselves!' Mama Rat said, glaring around the caravan. 'You're starting to worry the poor girl.' She leant forward on the bunk. 'The truth is, my dearie, that Gideon Plumpscuttle hates himself almost as much as he hates everyone around him. He is most unpleasant, but . . . there are worse owners, as I suspect you already know. At least he manages to keep us fed and housed, and he has yet to lay a hand on any of us . . .'

'If he ever does, I'll pound his head into a pancake,' muttered Gigantus.

'. . . and for the most part, he is hardly ever around. He takes the money we earn him and goes out every night to lose it all at cards or on dog fights, and then wastes the whole of the next day sleeping it off. And if you know how to handle him, he's a big pussycat.'

'To you, maybe,' said Gigantus, under his breath.

'It's true,' added Sister Moon. 'We do have a lot of time to ourselves. Plumpscuttle doesn't mind what we do, as long as we stay inside the house.'

Pyewacket pressed his face to the bars of his cage. 'Sitting around all day is dull as stinky ditchwater.'

'That's because you haven't found a hobby to occupy your mind,' said Gigantus, looking over the top of his journal.

'Actually, I think you'll find I have several *hobbies*.' Pyewacket looked down at Sheba and gave her a crooked smile. 'How would you like me to read your cards, hairy? Or your palm? Perhaps take a look at your tea leaves?'

Sheba swallowed. 'Are you . . . are you *really* a magical imp?'

'Of course he isn't!' Gigantus jumped in before Pyewacket could answer. 'He's barely even ten years old! He just *looks* like he was mixed up in a witch's cauldron, that's all.'

'Oi! You bulgy brute!' Pyewacket twisted his features into a hideous scowl, poking his tongue out at the big man. 'I've got more magic in my left nostril than you have in all those flopping great muscles! I'll prove it by telling this girl's fortune!'

'Um, maybe another time,' Sheba said, catching sight of the others frantically shaking their heads. 'But I can't believe you'd be bored. Aren't there hundreds of things to do in London? Sights to see, things to learn . . . and all the people.'

'All the unwashed beggars, you mean?'

'That's rich, coming from you, Wacket,' said Gigantus.

'Isn't London full of gentlefolk and royalty?' Sheba asked. She had imagined crowds of beautiful people popping in and out of Buckingham Palace for tea.

'There are many poor and needy,' said Sister Moon, after Pyewacket had stopped cackling. 'Some are very, very unfortunate.'

There was silence for a moment, as Sheba adjusted her mental picture of the big city. *Maybe it really isn't such a great place after all*, she thought, *even if it has got crystal palaces and giant cathedrals.*

'Well, it's lovely to meet you, Sheba,' said Mama Rat. 'I'm sure we'll all get along. But now, I think, that's enough chatting. It's time for bed.'

With a mixture of grunts and mumbles, the strange group began to ready themselves for sleep. Pyewacket wriggled around in his cage until he was somehow lying on his back, one of his stubby legs poking out of the open door. Mama Rat rested her head against her box of rats. Gigantus simply stretched himself out on the floor. Sister Moon curled at one end of Sheba's bunk.

Someone blew out the lantern, and the caravan was plunged into darkness, except for the glow of moonlight through its single, tiny window.

'Night, all,' said Mama Rat, and there was a chorus of replies. Not long after, a range of snores began: deep and rumbling; soft and smoky; high and reedy. Sheba thought she could place them all. She settled down into her mattress and was surprised to find herself feeling quite safe, despite her new surroundings and strange bedfellows.

In the darkness, a voice came from the end of the bunk.

'Are you all right, Sheba?' It was Sister Moon.

'I'm not sure,' Sheba replied. 'I mean, I think so. It's a lot to take in.'

'I felt the same when I first joined the show. Now I'm glad to be here. You'll be fine, don't worry.'

'Sister, can I ask you something?' There was a soft rustling sound, which may have been Sister Moon nodding. Sheba carried on. 'The others and I, we all look . . . strange somehow. But you're . . . *normal*. Aren't you?'

In answer, Sister Moon moved so that her face was caught in the moonlight. She motioned Sheba closer, then reached up to remove her smoke-lensed glasses.

Her eyelids were closed. Sheba noted the long, dark lashes, the elegant curve of her brows. She felt a twinge of jealousy, looking at the older girl's perfect, unblemished skin. *She's so beautiful*, Sheba thought. But then Sister Moon's eyes flicked open, and Sheba jumped back.

The sockets were hollow. Empty.

Or so they looked at first. When Sheba peered closer, she noticed light glinting on eyeballs. Her eyes were there, just jet black from one side to the other. Two pieces of polished obsidian, with no iris or pupil in sight.

'That's why I need the glasses,' Sister Moon said, slipping them back over her ears. 'I don't see very well in the daytime.'

'But at night?' Sheba asked.

'I see all.'

As a ray of moonlight lit up the caravan, Sheba saw that Sister Moon was smiling.

'Sweet dreams, Sheba,' she said. Then the moon slipped behind a cloud. Everything disappeared into darkness, and there were only the soft sounds of sleep.

*

When the grey morning light stirred Sheba, it took

her a moment to realise where she was. Her sleepy brain expected to be in her cage on the end of the pier. But instead of the fresh smell of the sea her nose was full of . . . the worst stink in the world. It was stronger than Mama Rat's stale pipe smoke, or the ratty pong that came from her wooden box; stronger even than the crusty stench of Pyewacket's trousers; and it was coming from outside the caravan.

She stood on her bunk and quietly levered open the tiny window, trying not to wake the others. It didn't reveal much except a view of hedgerows, the grey shire horse stomping moodily and Plumpscuttle dozing on the driving board. Sheba wriggled her head and shoulders through the opening to see more.

Fields and woodland stretched ahead of them, broken here and there by small clusters of houses. It looked almost exactly like the countryside she had trudged through with Plumpscuttle the day before – except for a sooty smudge on the horizon. A giant storm must be brewing; great billows of grey and black clouds were boiling in the air. But as Sheba looked closer, she could make out buildings and church spires among the blackness.

Then she realised what she was looking at.

London.

That enormous smear of smoke and stone was just one city, a colossal sprawl. Thousands upon thousands of buildings, and all of them filled with people. Her jaw hung open as she imagined the amount of brick, stone and wood needed to build such a thing. How could there be enough food in the world for all the hungry mouths inside it?

Sheba remained stuck, half in half out of the window, for the next hour, fascinated by the passing scenery. Quaint country houses rolled past; tiny thatched cottages with threads of white smoke drifting from the chimneys. Mile by mile, the view of London grew clearer. There was a hint of a great domed building that must be St Paul's Cathedral.[vii] She squinted, trying to get a glimpse of sparkling glass that might be the Exhibition's fabled palace made of crystal.

Soon there were clusters of houses, then small hamlets with their own inns and churches, followed by the junk mountains. Great heaps of rubbish and manure up to thirty feet high,[viii] each with a gaggle of rag-clad paupers climbing and rummaging in it. They passed the first factory she had ever seen, a looming cube of red brick with rows of tiny windows. Then there were more, reeking of leather, meat, brewing beer, hot iron and molten lead. Each had at least one chimney; all were belching out masses of black fumes. The stink stuck in her throat, burnt her lungs and made her cough. Lines of tattered workers turned to gawk at the strange, choking, hairy thing hanging out of the yellow caravan.

Sheba's sensitive nose was now burning. Not only was she smelling new odours at an alarming rate, but they were stronger, more powerful than anything she had smelled before. Her coughing turned to retching and her head began to spin. Clumps of black soot drifted into her face and flecked her hair. She tried to pull herself back into the caravan, away from the overpowering stench, but found she was stuck fast. Then a pair of massive hands closed around her ankles and yanked her inside. Through stinging eyes, she noticed the others were awake now, although there seemed to be more of them, swimming in and out of focus.

She opened her mouth to speak, but her head was so full of fumes she could barely think. 'The smell . . .' she managed to say, before she collapsed onto the bunk, unconscious.

*

The distant sound of a church clock striking echoed in Sheba's ears.

Ten? Eleven? But was it morning or night?

Peeling open an eyelid, she saw daylight. Morning, then.

She had been under for a few hours and, thankfully, her brain had used the time to adjust itself to London's stench.

The smells that had knocked her out were now dimmed to a background noise, thrumming in her nose. She tried to list them: smoke, burning. Rotting meat, blocked drains. Gas, of some sort. And sewage. Lots and lots of sewage.

Sitting up, she discovered she was lying on a pile of tatty blankets in a small, square room. Plaster crumbled from the walls and, next to her, there was a window that looked out onto a street of squashed houses, pavements thronged with people. Around her were a collection of other beds and the box that held Mama Rat's 'darlings'. Tiny rodent snores drifted from within. Someone had left her little ebony box by her side. A quick check told her everything was still in its place.

At one end of the room was a door from which strange noises were leaking. It sounded as if a herd of pigs were trying to gargle syrup. By the smell, she supposed it was Plumpscuttle, fast asleep and snoring.

At the other end of the room was a staircase. She padded down it, emerging into an almost bare parlour with a simple fireplace and a single rickety armchair. Next door was a kitchen with a splintered table and chairs fashioned out of old tea crates. The window was open, but Sheba was too small to peep over the sill. Instead, she opened the back door and stepped out to see a bizarre sight.

In the far corner of a dusty, fenced yard was the yellow caravan. The opposite corner held a small privy shed and a squat iron cage from which Pyewacket's face was currently peeking. A gate stood open to the street beyond and on it, in flourishing but faded script, Sheba read, '*Carnival of the Lost. Misfits, Oddments and Monstrosities. Terror and Amazement await you. Entry 1d.*'

All would have seemed quite normal, if it wasn't for the giant grey shire horse in the middle of the yard, stalking back and forth with an evil glint in its eyes. That, and the figures who were trying to shepherd it into a stall next to the house.

'Come on, Raggety dearie. Good horsey,' crooned Mama Rat.

The horse gnashed its teeth in her direction, and she skipped backward.

Sheba hadn't seen many horses, but she was pretty sure they weren't supposed to scowl like that.

'Don't get too close,' warned Sister Moon. She was poised just outside the horse's striking distance, ready to leap to safety.

'Get in the stall, you manky old nag, or I'll pound you into glue,' said Gigantus, bravely, but even he was keeping well away from the horse's back hooves.

Raggety made a deep rumbling noise that

sounded almost like a growl.

Sheba took a handful of sugar cubes from the bowl on the kitchen windowsill and walked slowly forward, holding out her offering. 'Here, Raggety,' she whispered. She didn't know much about animals – except for Flossy, of course – but all creatures responded better to kindness, she reckoned. That, and a spot of bribery.

The horse eyed her suspiciously, then edged forward and nibbled at the sugar. Despite looking as though he wanted to eat her hand as well, he was surprisingly gentle. He crunched the sweet granules, eyes closed in pleasure.

Sheba slowly backed away, towards the stall. 'Come on, Raggety, there's a good boy,' she murmured.

Whickering under his breath, the horse clopped towards her. He knew he was being tricked, but it would be worth it for more of that delicious white stuff.

Step by step, Sheba led Raggety into his stall, keeping him entranced by the sugar until Gigantus had closed the gate. As Sheba stroked Raggety's long grey mane, she noticed Flossy's basket was standing nearby. She guessed he was going to live here too. He gave her a nervous double bleat, and she kneeled to give his heads a reassuring pat. The journey to London seemed to have perked him up a bit, although maybe he was just relieved to get away from Grunchgirdle. Hopefully he would be happier in his new home. As long as Raggety didn't squish him into jelly.

Sheba fed Raggety the rest of the sugar, then clambered out.

'Well done, Sheba!' said Mama Rat, slapping her on the back. The rats squeaked in a rodent form of applause.

Sheba felt a strange, warm tingle flow through her. It felt surprisingly good to be able to help someone.

'Aye, good lass, that would have taken us hours,' said Gigantus.

'Clever, Sheba! Do you feel better now?' asked Sister Moon.

For the first time, Sheba noticed Sister Moon had two knives strapped to her belt, the handles visible beneath her open jacket. Big knives, with blades that must have been as long as Sheba's forearms.

'Yes. Yes, thank you,' muttered Sheba, wondering what such weapons might be for. 'It's just this place . . . this city. I've never smelled anything like it.'

'Make sure you steer clear of Pyewacket on a hot day, then,' said Gigantus, chuckling.

A muffled stream of insults began to pour from the rusty cage in the corner, but they were cut off by a deafening, gargling snort from the upstairs window.

'Come on, you lot, there's work to do before Plumpscuttle wakes up,' said Mama Rat.

'What kind of work?' Sheba asked.

Gigantus pointed to a stack of rope and sheets and paper lanterns. 'We've got to get that lot up by sundown.'

'And then what?' asked Sheba.

'Showtime,' said Sister Moon, smiling.

CHAPTER THREE

In which Sheba goes back on show,
and makes a mysterious friend.

Night fell on the city. Gas lamps lit the streets with a flickering yellow glow, and orange candlelight twinkled everywhere. Peeking out of the bedroom window, Sheba looked down on a scene of enchantment. Brick Lane had been transformed into a fairy city.

The pavements were full of ballad singers,[ix] jugglers, stilt-walkers and hawkers selling dodgy pies – some still with the odd feather or tail poking out. Among them milled the scruffy poor of the East End, along with a handful of rich folk who must have wandered down from the city to sample the slums for their amusement. These were prime targets for the hordes of sneaking pickpockets who scurried like ants through the crowd, dipping for purses, watches and silk handkerchiefs.

This, thought Sheba, was how she imagined a city, all those years she was shut up at Grunchgirdle's. A place full of noise and bustle and life. Just as fascinating as Mama Rat had said it would be, as long as you didn't breathe through your nose.

The front door to the house was wide open, with signs propped outside advertising the wonders within. Plumpscuttle's lazy nephew, Phineas, stood with a money box and a roll of tickets, beckoning in punters without much enthusiasm.

Sheba marvelled at the transformation. A hard afternoon's work hanging sheets from the ceiling had turned the dingy little rooms into a maze of corridors and tiny chambers. The coloured paper lanterns gave the place an eerie glow, as if it were some kind of fairy kingdom, rather than a run-down brick shack. Arrows and pointing fingers painted on scraps of cardboard showed the audience the route, and signs on the walls promised terrors, delights and amazement in equal measure.

Sheba could hear Plumpscuttle in the parlour. She peeked down the staircase. He was standing on a box, lit by a ring of candles which made his hair glow fiery orange. Having slept off his long night of travel, he was letting rip with a mighty speech about the glories of his sideshow. His cheeks throbbed like two beetroots as he shouted. He only had a small crowd, but he was giving it his all.

Behind him, Mama Rat had turned the contents of her box into a miniature big top. The wooden crate had unfolded into a perfect, tiny circus. There were trapezes, a tightrope, hoops and tunnels, all painted in bright diamonds of red and yellow. Waiting in the wings were six enormous rats, their names printed on their little velvet collars: Bartholomew, Matthew, Judas, Thaddeus, Simon and Peter. They had been squeezed into hand-sewn miniature circus outfits trimmed with gold braid: clowns, acrobats and even a ringmaster. And, although the costumes did nothing to hide their yellow teeth, glinting eyes and thick, scaly tails,

Sheba had to admit they looked almost charming.

As the punters gathered around, the rats tumbled out into the circus ring and began performing a range of tricks. At the merest nod or wink from Mama Rat they turned somersaults, did backflips and balanced on top of one another in a teetering pyramid. Sheba grinned.

Behind the partition, Sister Moon soon had a crowd of seven or more. Sheba peeked through a hole in the blanket as the audience gathered. She watched as Moon took off her top hat and bowed, slowly removing her glasses to show her blank, empty eyes.

The audience gasped. And then she stepped towards the lantern, blowing it out with a puff. Sheba could almost hear the audience's hearts pounding as the cubicle was plunged into darkness. It was only for a split second. A heartbeat or less. Until, on the far side, a match was struck, and Sister Moon was revealed, clutching an armful of hats, handkerchiefs, silk scarves and bonnets. Somehow, she had moved from one end of the room to the other – quicker than a blink – and had stripped her audience of their belongings as she went.

Faster than the light, indeed.

The audience cheered as she handed back their things, and Sheba couldn't help clapping too. One gentleman started to make a fuss about being 'robbed', but Moon simply allowed her jacket to fall open, revealing one of the long hunting knives that hung at her belt.[x] After that, the gentleman was very, very quiet.

And that explains the blades, Sheba thought.

But she couldn't gawk for long. The next stop for the customers was her corner of the bedroom. Inspired by the rest of the carnival troupe, she dashed back to her stool and sat patiently as a line of people filed slowly past. She tried not to listen as they made noises of disgust or horror, and instead concentrated on her own act: being as wolfish as possible. She widened her eyes so they glinted orange in the lantern light, and let her sharp white teeth poke out. But it was a while since she'd had to sit for a customer, and it was hard to listen to their comments after the applause for Mama Rat and Sister Moon:

'Poor thing!' a woman said.

'What a sight!' her friend muttered.

'Do you think she combs her body?' asked a third.

Sheba sighed. She'd moved halfway across the country, but her life had changed very little.

Out in the yard, Sheba could hear gasps of amazement as a bare-chested Gigantus lifted a wooden bench. It happened to have three fully grown men sitting on it, and he hoisted it over his head as if it were a sack of feathers. She didn't hear anyone calling him names.

Behind his colossal shoulders was Pyewacket's cage. He had dressed himself in a robe and hat, daubed all over with mysterious symbols. A sign stood beside the cage, describing his magical origins and offering free fortune-telling. The few people who had dared to wander over were listening to nonsense about stars and planets, and were then cursed loudly when they walked away, laughing.

Flossy was out there somewhere, too. On display in his pen, ready for people to prod, poke and stare at. She hoped he was all right. At least Raggety would be near, ready to chomp the fingers of anyone who got too close.

Sister Moon popped her head around the sheet partition.

'Is your show going well, Sheba?'

Sheba nodded, smiling back. It was the first time anyone had ever checked on her during a performance. For once she felt like she wasn't completely on her own. Others were going through this ordeal with her. She was part of something bigger than herself. It was a small gesture, but it made her indescribably happy. She forgot about looking beastly and beamed instead.

The next group of punters was very disappointed.

'What's this supposed to be, then?'

'It's just a young girl sitting on a chair.'

'My missus looks worse first thing in the mornin'!'

Sheba strained her hardest, willing her snout to twitch, her fangs to jut, but she could feel her features remaining stubbornly normal. Trying another approach, she instead imagined Grunchgirdle with his bony, shaking fingers and watery, spiteful eyes. She pictured the way he used to poke her through the cage bars with a broom handle, how he cursed at her and called her 'freak' and 'monster': all the cruel humiliations she had endured over the years.

It was as if the wolf inside her suddenly woke. With a snarl, her eyes flashed, her jaw stretched and her teeth snapped. She dropped onto all fours, growling. From girl to animal in the blink of an eye.

Her audience yelped, and rushed back through the sheets and down the stairs, leaving her alone again.

Sheba sat quietly growling, until she noticed that not quite all of them had gone. In front of her was a little girl, wide-eyed and clutching at her pinafore, but standing her ground.

'Sorry,' said Sheba, sitting back on her stool. She suddenly felt very self-conscious and ashamed. With a blink, her amber eyes returned to normal, and she hid her sharp teeth behind a pout.

'That was very good,' said the girl. She gave Sheba a shy smile. 'Bit scary, though.'

'Sorry,' Sheba said again. 'I didn't mean to frighten you.'

''S all right,' said the girl.

Sheba looked at her visitor properly. She was stick-thin and pale as a dead fish, the bones of her skull pushing through her skin. Dark shadows ringed her eyes and, beneath her patched pinafore, she wore rags that were crusted with stale mud. Her feet were bare and covered with angry-looking welts and scratches. *This must be one of those unfortunate people Sister Moon was talking about*, Sheba thought. Could she be one of the scavengers from the dust heaps? Or somewhere even worse?

'Do you live in London?' It was a silly question, but Sheba didn't know what to say. She'd never spoken to her audience before.

'Yes, down by the river.' The girl smiled again. 'Me ma will never believe me when I tells her about you and the others!'

'Is this the first time you've been to the show?'

'First time I've been anywhere in town,' the girl said. 'I'm supposed to be out on the river, picking from the mud, but I didn't feel like it. Went for a walk instead.'

Sheba was about to ask what strange kind of fruit would need picking from a stinking riverbank, when the girl took something from her pocket and held it out to her. Sheba looked. It was a chipped glass marble, the size of a small pebble and bottle green.

She placed it in Sheba's hand.

'My name's Till,' said the girl. She watched as Sheba rolled the marble between her fingers. 'You can keep that if you like. Picked it up this morning.'

'Thank you,' said Sheba, genuinely touched. It was the first time she could remember being given anything. She was filled with gratitude, but guilty too, as she had nothing to share in return.

Instead she offered her name. 'I'm Sheba.'

Till opened her mouth to say more, when the thunderous boom of Plumpscuttle's voice echoed up from below.

'What do you mean, she sneaked past without paying? Get off your lazy backside and find her, you dolt! And then bring her to me so I can kick her back where she came from!'

'I've got to go!' Till rushed to the hanging sheets and peeped through.

'Didn't you get a ticket?' asked Sheba.

'Nah, I ran past that simple cove on the door. Think I can afford a penny?' She put her eye back to the gap in the sheet. The thumping feet of Phineas Plumpscuttle came up the stairs towards Sheba's partition. Till scuttled under the sheets, past Sister Moon and down the stairs, just as Phineas peered round to where Sheba was sitting.

'Oi, you. Have you seen a muddy little urchin in here? Uncle wants to hit her.'

'Haven't seen anyone,' Sheba lied.

As Phineas drifted off to look elsewhere, she rubbed the chipped glass of the marble with her thumb and imagined herself playing with Till on the riverbank. As if she were just an ordinary child.

CHAPTER FOUR

Which mostly smells of rancid river mud,
but with a dash of added terror.

Till smiled – she had been out picking for almost an hour and had found a few scraps of metal, half a clay pipe and a brown bottle with a mouthful of gin still swilling in the bottom. A good morning's work. Enough to sell on the street later for a penny or two, which in turn would buy a morsel for supper.

The handful of treasures clanked together in the hessian sack at her side as she pulled one foot out of the clingy mud and took another step forward. The river bed released a small cloud of green gas, then closed up again, swallowing her footprint: as if she had never been there.

She had wrapped her bare feet with rags. Broken glass and rusty nails were hidden in the slime like sixpences in an evil Christmas pudding. You couldn't be too careful: one cut might mean blood poisoning and a lingering, miserable death.

Somewhere to the left she could hear the distant *suck-slop-suck-slop* of her elder brother, trudging in the same awkward way. She would have been able to see him too, if it wasn't for the blanket of mist obscuring everything.

London fog was unlike any other. It seeped into your nostrils, your eyes, even your skin; stinging and burning and choking. It poured down the narrow streets, sat heavy on the leaning rooftops. The whole river, the whole city, could be rubbed out of sight by the white wall of nothing. And today it was thicker than ever.

Till shivered, but kept her eyes fixed on the lumpy surface of the mud. Her mind kept drifting back to the night before, when she had snuck into the sideshow on Brick Lane. Her left ear still throbbed from where her father had clipped her when he'd heard what she'd done. Not for sneaking in without paying, but for wandering off when she should have been making the most of low tide. *We can't afford to miss a chance to pick*, he'd said, for the hundredth time. Not that Till cared. It had been more than worth it to see those bizarre people, and to meet that little girl. Just like her, but covered in hair. And those teeth and claws! *If only I had something strange about me*, she thought, *then I could sit in a sideshow like a queen and have people pay to look at me, instead of having to wade through stinking slime.*

She was just picturing herself with a pair of feathered wings, starring in a famous circus somewhere, when, out of the corner of her eye, she saw a ripple in the silt.

There wasn't much still alive in the Thames, apart from an eel or two.[xi] Great, long, slithery things, grown fat on the bodies of unfortunate folk that had died in the river, if her nan was to be believed. But that didn't bother Till. All she was thinking right now was that there might be something in the mud worth eating. Something that would make a change from cabbage water and gruel.

With her hungry tongue poking between her lips she rounded on the source of the ripple. Slowly, slowly, so as not to scare it, she crouched and eased her way through the mud. Her feet made soft slurps as they broke the surface and slipped back down into the clammy ooze.

When she reached the spot where the movement had been, she stopped and held her breath. She stood motionless for what seemed like an age. Nothing stirred, and for a moment she thought she might have imagined the whole thing. Then it came again. A shudder in the brown, porridgey gloop, somewhere near the surface.

Till's hands shot into the mud like lightning. She felt the long, slimy body of the eel between her fingers, and closed them around it. Her grip was as tight and hard as the hunger in her empty little belly. The eel didn't want to budge, but she gritted her teeth and pulled, until her hands broke free of the water. Gripped between them was a fat, wiggling creature, wet and slimy. Till's face broke into a wide grin. It was massive!

She continued to heave, her mind racing with thoughts of eel pie, eel soup, eel casserole with extra eel.

More and more of the creature inched up, heaved out of the slime.

Till dug her heels in. Any minute now the head would break free and she could knock the thing's brains out with her bottle and drag it back home for dinner.

She started to haul, hand over hand, but there was still no sign of it ever stopping . . .

It was about then that Till's skin began to prickle, that she realised that the eel wasn't quite normal. The ones she had seen at the fish market had been a grey-green colour; as sickly-looking as the river water they'd been hooked from. This one was bright red. And smooth all the way down. No gills, no fins, no head . . .

As she stared down at it, the fog around her seemed to thicken, and the eel began to thrash unnaturally from side to side. Till let go with a shriek. She fell backward, smack, into the stinking silt.

But the eel was still moving. Even though she was no longer pulling it, the thing was rising upwards.

'What the jibbins are you?' Till managed to shout, although it came out as more of a squeak.

All around her, the mud was heaving itself up now, as something pushed its way to the surface.

Till started to slide backward through the muck, her legs pedalling furiously as she tried to find purchase in the slime. Whatever was about to burst out from the riverbed, she didn't want to be around to see it.

With a sucking, slurping sound an enormous domed carapace emerged, studded with spikes. Till got a glimpse of one saucer-sized yellow eye and a pair of long grasping claws.

She screamed and flipped onto her front, scrabbling, crawling, stumbling away from the hellish thing.

A cold, hard, serrated pincer clasped her ankle and pulled. The chilly mud slurped as it swallowed her legs, her waist, her chest. The stinking jelly crept up her cheeks, slithering over her clenched lips, her closed eyes.

She fought to raise a hand, waving, clutching, calling out to her brother . . . hoping that he – or anyone – might see her and come to the rescue . . . but they didn't.

And then it was over.

The fog whirled for a moment, before settling back into a wall of blank grey. The splatters and splashes on the mud gradually melted away, like a wound healing. Every sign of the terrible struggle was erased. The only clue that Till had even existed was her tattered picking sack. That, and an echo of her last shriek drifting along the river.

CHAPTER FIVE

In which the carnival receives some desperate visitors.

Breakfast was a cup of weak coffee, served at the kitchen table. Sheba peered over the rim of her chipped mug at the others sitting around the cramped room. Mama Rat sipped tea in between puffs of her pipe. Gigantus was writing away again, his pencil looping across the paper. Sister Moon, missing her glasses for once, sat with her eyes closed, deep in thought.

'What are you doing?' Sheba asked her.

'Meditating,' said Moon, eyes still closed. 'My mother is from Hong Kong, and I grew up there. We are Buddhists, and this is how we focus our minds. Praying, you would call it.'

'Buddhists?'

'It's a religion.' Sister Moon opened one ebony eye a fraction and smiled. Sheba was itching to ask her more about her past, how she had ended up in the carnival, but didn't want to seem nosy. Perhaps when they knew each other a little better.

She noticed someone was missing from the room. 'Where's Pyewacket?'

'He's not allowed out of his cage,' said Sister Moon.

'Plumpscuttle doesn't let him in the house,' added Gigantus. 'Ever since he cursed him with boils on his bottom.'

'That was unpleasant for all concerned,' said Mama Rat, shaking her head.

'Is the boss back, then?' asked Sheba. After last night's show, he had gone out and she hadn't heard him return, nor the gargling snoring from his room.

'He'll be back soon,' said Sister Moon. Keeping her eyes closed, she put a spoonful of sugar in her coffee, stirred it, then lifted the cup and took a sip.

'And in an awful mood too,' said Mama Rat. 'Out all night, his money gone and sick as a pig. But he'll probably go straight to bed and sleep until evening. We'll just try to keep out of his way.'

As Mama was speaking, Sheba caught a familiar whiff through the open kitchen window. Stale sweat and pie crust. She marvelled at how her nose could still pick out a scent among the London stink.

'He's almost here,' she said.

The others looked at her as if she were mad, but then the front door slammed open with enough force to shake plaster from the rafters. Heavy footsteps boomed across the parlour, and Plumpscuttle's purple, blotchy face appeared at the kitchen door.

'Get me some chuffing coffee!' he roared to no one in particular.

Mama Rat filled and held out a mug. Plumpscuttle snatched it and drained the contents in one gulp, spilling half of it down his front. Then he glowered at them all.

'I'm going to bed – don't you lot dare make a sound.'

He clomped upstairs, and his bedroom door

slammed shut. A few moments later, a sound like a walrus being strangled drifted through the floorboards.

'That's him out for the day,' said Gigantus, still writing away.

'How did you know he was coming, Sheba?' asked Sister Moon, a delicate eyebrow raised.

'I smelled him,' she said.

'I must say, he is a bit on the ripe side,' said Mama Rat, 'but that is a very extraordinary skill you have, my dearie.'

Sheba felt a blush creep under her fur. She wasn't used to being paid compliments. Thankfully Sister Moon changed the subject.

'Shall we wake Pyewacket?'

'If we must.' Gigantus gave a sigh.

They all headed out into the yard. After stopping to check on Flossy – who was actually making an attempt to frolic – and trying to give Raggety some sugar without losing a hand, Sheba joined the others at the cage in the corner. Mama Rat yanked the door open and gave Pyewacket a prod. 'Come on, dearie, morning time.'

There was a rustling from the straw within, then a boy-sized object burst out and began tumbling around the yard. He clambered up on top of the privy and gurned down at the others below him.

'Finally!' He made a show of stretching his limbs. 'My arms were getting cramp in there!'

Sheba marvelled as he flexed his long arms. They were almost twice as long as his body, thick and roped with muscle.

'They'd get cramp if you slept in a cowshed,' said Gigantus.

'Watch out,' said Pyewacket, grinning wide enough to display all his yellow tusks. 'I might reach one into your room when you're asleep and pluck out one of your many nose hairs. Then I'll use it to put a spell on you. I'll make you think you're a ballerina, me old china.'

'Just you try it,' said Gigantus, with a growl.

Rather than being scared, Pyewacket rolled about on the privy roof, hooting with laughter. And Sheba couldn't help but giggle herself.

*

The bells of Christ Church struck four in the afternoon. Mama Rat was leaning against one of the caravan's large wooden wheels, reading a copy of *The Times*. Pyewacket was casting a handful of bones on the ground over and over, staring at them and muttering about omens and portents. Gigantus was scribbling away once more, pausing every now and then to stare into space and chew his pencil, and Sister Moon was throwing those long hunting knives of hers at a wooden pole. Her hands snatched them from their scabbards in a blur, then they whirled end over end before *thunking* into their targets. She had just managed to split a fly clean in half.

Sheba sat on an old milking stool, feeling bored. This was hardly the exciting big-city life she had been expecting. Perhaps the days of sitting at the end of Little Pilchton pier hadn't been that dull after all.

About an hour ago, she'd had the idea of creating a scent map of London. A list of the distinct odours in each place that she could use to find her way around if she ever got lost.

Brick Lane. That was the first entry. *Pie shops, rubbish heaps. Rotting wood, roasted coffee and chimney smoke.* And then, the smell of the house. *Rodents' droppings, horse manure and Flossy. Plumpscuttle's dirty laundry and Mama Rat's pipe smoke. Pyewacket.*

But, without being able to travel anywhere else, that was as far as she'd got.

Sheba sighed. 'Can I read some of your newspaper, please, Mama Rat?' she asked. At least now she didn't have to squirrel articles away in Flossy's pen. She smiled when the woman handed her the front page.

The headlines were all about the Great Exhibition. There was a report about a group of seven hundred farmers who had travelled up from the country, a review of the latest exhibits from America and an article moaning about how awful the food was. There were etchings of the most amazing attractions: the Koh-i-noor diamond ('the largest in the world!'), the pink crystal fountain ('twenty-seven feet high!') and Mr Faraday's revolutionary electromagnetic engine ('like captured lightning!'). It seemed as if the Exhibition was the only thing the city was talking about.

'Have any of you been to see the Great Exhibition

in the palace of crystal?'

'It's the *Crystal Palace*, dearie,' said Mama Rat. 'And no, we have not as yet had the pleasure.'

'They probably wouldn't let the likes of us in,' said Pyewacket. 'Not unless we offered to be part of the show.'

'It would take an entire day to queue up, see the sights and get home again,' said Mama Rat. 'Plumpscuttle would notice we were gone, and *then* there'd be trouble.'

'Well, *I'd* like to see it,' Sheba said to herself.

'Me too,' said Sister Moon. 'We'll go together some time.'

Sheba blushed – she'd thought her comment was too quiet to be heard – and then nodded at Sister Moon. *This must be what having a friend is like*, she thought. A proper one, with a single head and no fleece.

She was imagining herself and Moon, strolling through the glass corridors among the glorious exhibits, when there was a knock on the yard door.

The carnival acts stared at each other in surprise for a few seconds. Then the more shocking of them rushed to hide, so as not to frighten off their visitors. Gigantus lumbered into the house, Sheba slid under the old caravan and Pyewacket hopped back in his cage, burying himself under the straw.

Sister Moon stood like a palace guard next to Mama Rat, who arranged herself on a bench and called out, 'Please enter!'

The gate swung open and, with much shuffling of feet and backward glances, two figures entered the yard. A woman and a man. From her hiding place, Sheba could see they were bent and tattered – the poorest of the poor. They were wearing nothing more than rags held together with patches. Their skin was stretched tight over bone. Underneath a filthy shawl and what might once have been a hat, wide eyes flicked around the yard. The dried mud caking their feet reminded Sheba of Till, the girl at the show last night.

'Good day,' said Mama Rat, beaming at them from her seat. 'Excuse the messy yard, but it's not often we have company. How can we be helping you?'

There was a flurry of nudging and shoving, until finally the man was pushed forward a step. He removed his threadbare cap and stared at the ground in front of Mama Rat's feet. When he spoke, Sheba was startled to hear a young man's voice. He looked almost ancient. *What a harsh life these people must lead to age them so*, she thought.

'If you please,' he said. 'We 'as come to see you, as nobody else 'as even given us the time of day. We've been all over Sarf London asking for 'elp, and been spat on as often as not. We 'ad all but given up 'ope, until the missus fought of asking yourselves.'

'Help, dearie?' said Mama Rat. 'I think you've got us mistaken. We're just a small carnival troupe. Unless you want to book us for a performance, we won't be much use to you.'

The woman plucked up courage and stepped forward to speak. She too sounded much younger than she looked.

'It's our little girl, ma'am. She came 'ere last night; told us all about you lot and how fantastic and magical you all were. Then she went out to gather from the south bank of the river this morning, near the East Lane Stairs, like always. But she never come back. All we found is 'er picking sack, left on the mud . . . My poor Till . . .' The woman broke down in tears.

From her hiding place beneath the caravan, Sheba gasped. Till!

'Missing, you say?' said Mama Rat. 'And you're sure she hasn't just run away?'

'Run away to what?' asked the man, then looked shocked at his sudden outburst. 'Begging your pardon, but you can see from the sight of us that we 'as no better station to run to than the one we got. Picking from the mud is all we is good for. Ain't nowhere else for us, nor no one what would have us. Not in this city, anyways.'

'I am very sorry for it,' said Mama Rat, 'but you have a point. I'm afraid I have nothing to tell you, though. I didn't even know she had been here. There was quite a crowd, you see. Has she failed to come home before?'

The ragged man shook his head. 'No, ma'am. Besides skipping off to see you lot last night, she's always done as she was told. Tess thought she might 'ave come back to join you, but I said, "What's fantastical about a raggedy little mudlark?" Folk like you wouldn't want someone like 'er hanging around . . .'

Mama Rat sat and puffed on her pipe for a few moments while the mudlark woman sniffled and the man twitched his cap.

Sheba reached forward and clutched the wheel spokes, staring wide-eyed from the shadows. She felt an urge to rush out into the streets, to start searching for poor, helpless Till immediately. But it was pointless. She still didn't know the first thing about London. She'd be lost in seconds.

But we have to help find her, we just have to! She could almost picture Till – lost and lonely somewhere, away from her parents. It was hard enough for Sheba, forever wondering about the family she had never had. Imagine having known that kind of love and having it ripped away from you.

The others, though . . . they knew London. They might have a clue where to find her.

Say we'll help! She tried to will the thought across the yard and into Mama Rat's head. *Don't just send them away!* She would have jumped out and begged, if she didn't think it would send Till's parents screaming out of the yard.

In between the clouds of pipe smoke, Mama Rat caught her eye. Some kind of understanding passed between them.

'I think,' she said, pausing for a thoughtful puff, 'if you wanted, that is . . . that we might be able to help find her.'

'You will?' The man looked directly at Mama Rat for the first time, his mouth open in shock. 'You really will?'

'I'm not promising anything,' said Mama Rat. 'As I said, we're just a humble carnival troupe. But we do have some connections and . . . abilities that might be of service, I suppose. And after all, your daughter was a member of our audience, however briefly.'

'Lawd bless you,' said the man, clapping his hands. From under her spatterings of dirt and grime, the woman beamed with relief. 'And we'll pay you all back some'ow. Even if it takes us fifty years of sifting mud, we will.'

At that moment a large amount of banging and shouting could be heard coming from the upstairs window of the house. Plumpscuttle was stirring.

'Yes, yes, we'll discuss all that later,' said Mama Rat, panicking a little. Sister Moon stepped forward and began ushering the mudpickers towards the gate. 'We'll send word when we have any information for you. Keep your ears open, and please feel free to visit again, should you discover anything yourselves. Good afternoon, dearies!'

''Ang on a minute—' the man began to say, but Sister Moon's firm grip had sent the pair into the street. The gate was already closing on them.

Moments later, the back door of the house banged open and that bleary lump, Plumpscuttle, appeared.

'Did I just see some people in my yard?' he bellowed. 'Some strange folk, uninvited on my personal property? Some scrawny street-offal covered in rags and filthy muck?'

'We were just asking them if they knew anyone selling good food,' said Sheba, as she climbed out from under the caravan. 'We were all feeling a bit peckish.'

'Peckish? You lot don't know what the word means! I could eat that scrawny two-headed sheep raw! Get me five helpings of whatever you're having. And make it quick.' He threw a handful of copper pennies out into the yard, then stomped off into the house.

Mama Rat gave Sheba a thoughtful look as Sister Moon scooped up the money and headed off to the butcher's shop.

'You, young lady, are beginning to prove immensely useful,' she said.

*

Sheba liked the idea of dumping Plumpscuttle's dinner in front of him and then dashing down to the river to begin the hunt for Till, but, as Sister Moon explained, they had a show to put on later, and after that it would be too dark to see anything. Sadly, the search would have to wait for morning.

As a consolation, she found herself presented with a bowl of penny dip: fried sheep heart and liver, mixed with onions and dumplings. To Sheba it tasted exotic and delicious, even if the dumplings were quite gritty.[xii] She tried not to look at Flossy as she smacked her lips over each mouthful.

The others shovelled it down without expression. When you had the same food every single day, it was difficult to get excited about it.

They ate outside, sitting cross-legged on the yard floor, as Plumpscuttle had claimed the kitchen table. Every now and then the sound of a wet burp echoed through the window.

'So,' said Gigantus. 'What do you make of them mud-grubblers?'

'Bad news,' said Pyewacket. 'I can feel it in my bunions. There's a black cloud of ill omen hanging over them. Just look at their pinched faces and poxy skin. And they haven't got two ha'pennies to rub together, neither.'

'I recall your start to life wasn't that much better, half pint,' said Gigantus, as he licked the last bit of gravy from his spoon.

'That's got nothing to do with it!' Pyewacket shouted, spraying everyone with a mouthful of half-chewed sheep guts. 'All I'm saying is, there's no point in helping such as them out! Don't you know how many people there are in this city? Theirs is just one more sad story in a city of two million. Their daughter probably got sucked down a mud-hole. Or met a cockroach who carried her off to be his wife.'

'That little girl,' said Sheba, 'happens to be my friend. Her name is Till, and she was very sweet and kind to me. Unlike most people. If there's a way to help her, then I will.'

Pyewacket fell quiet, staring at Sheba with his yellow eyes.

'Well said, dearie.' Mama Rat gave Sheba a wink. 'Those better off should always try and help the less fortunate. That's why I agreed on behalf of us all. And my clever rattie darlings will come in useful, looking for that girl.'

'In what way?' Sheba couldn't think how a miniature circus would be any help in finding a missing mudlark.

'Oh, my boys are very good at detecting things. They can go from one end of this city to the other without anyone so much as catching a whiff of them. They've found all sorts of bits and pieces for me over the years. All sorts indeed.'

CHAPTER SIX

In which the hunt for Till begins.

The best place to look for Till, they decided, was where she had last been seen. Near the East Lane Stairs on the south bank of the Thames.

And so, early the next morning, they'd set off, Sheba following Gigantus, one little furry hand clutching the back of his jersey as he steamed through the early morning throng like an icebreaker. *Then* it had seemed marvellous and exhilarating to be out and about in the big city, but the novelty had soon worn off.

At Bermondsey waterfront, the tanneries were already pumping streams of thick red fluid into the river: a mixture of chemicals, acid and waste – it let out fumes that could take your eyebrows off at fifty paces. At the tannery doors, a steady stream of poo-pickers had begun to gather, clutching steaming pails: the leather works needed excrement for tanning the hides and each carried a bucket of fresh dog droppings that they had collected from the streets. They guarded them as if they contained pure gold, rather than wet, stinking mess.

Sheba tugged her hood over her head, hiding her face in its shadows. Her nose was completely swamped by the disgusting aromas.

Another entry for my scent map, she thought. *Bermondsey: the worst smell ever invented.*

They had been here since dawn, nearly an hour ago, asking anyone they could persuade to stop and speak to them about Till, the missing mudlark. Sheba's hopes had been high, but nobody seemed to know anything. Or rather, they didn't want to answer questions from such a strange bunch of snoopers.

Only Gigantus had been getting any results. When he stepped in front of someone it was like being confronted by a small mountain. People stood trembling while he asked about the lost girl, then told him every scrap of information they thought could be valuable, and often more besides. He currently loomed over a trembling bargeman who was babbling about some spoons hidden under his bedroom floorboards. The others were leaning up against the dock wall, looking out over the river.

Since the sun had first begun to strain through the dawn smog, boats had been rowing, sailing and steaming up and down it. A splendid three-masted clipper was now gliding its way to the Pool of London, making the tiny skiffs and wherries around it seem like floating insects.

Something about its majestic lines and jutting prow stirred a feeling in Sheba. A memory, perhaps, but fluttering just beyond her reach: another loose thread. Had she ever been on a ship? She didn't think so. But she could tell which bit was the bow, which the stern. She knew the deck would roll under your feet when the waves were high, that the ropes creaked, that sailors climbed so high in the rigging, they looked like specks up above . . .

But how?

It was like the familiar dream. Her bare, hairless feet slapping on the cold marble as she ran through the white house. Had these things ever really happened to her? Or were they fragments of nightmares? Pieces of leftover imaginings, stuck in her brain like fish bones between her teeth.

That was the most likely explanation. At least for a girl who was probably dumped at the doorstep of the orphanage by some starving pauper, struck dumb with horror at the hairy child she had given birth to.

Just thinking of it all made Sheba's head swim. A hundred different emotions at once: anger at being abandoned; shame at being so different; sorrow for whoever had been desperate enough to abandon their own child. Old feelings that were best left deep inside. She banished them there now, turning her eyes away from the clipper and onto the Thames itself.

Beneath all the boats and steamers, beneath the oozing brown water and the floating lumps of *stuff* that swirled in it, was the mud that Till had spent her life combing for treasure. In her cape pocket, Sheba ran her fingers over the cracked green marble. *Is she down there now?* she wondered. *Did she get sucked under that cold, clammy muck? Or did someone take her from the river to a different place entirely?*

They were upsetting thoughts, but Sheba couldn't help them. Pyewacket was right: in a city teeming with so many people, what were the chances of finding one lost girl?

'There's some more of the bony goblins.' As if he had heard Sheba think his name, Pyewacket spoke up. He pointed his finger at a pack of tattered children who were lounging beside a set of stone stairs, waiting for the tide to ebb. 'Is one of them mudlarks this Till girl?'

Sheba scanned them quickly, but none of them looked like her friend. 'No.' She sighed. 'But maybe we could ask them about her?'

'Good thinking,' said Mama Rat. 'They might have seen where she disappeared.'

But as the troupe began to clamber down to the greasy sliver of exposed riverbank, the mudlarks saw them coming and, in a blink, they were lost among the bustle of the docks.

'Ha! You 'ave to be quicker than that to catch 'em!'

What Sheba had taken to be a mound of grubby sacking and torn fishing nets moved and spoke. It was an old woman with a bird's nest of grey hair and wrinkles packed with so much dirt they looked like lines inked on leathery parchment.

'We don't mean them any harm,' said Sister Moon, touching the brim of her top hat in greeting. 'We're searching for a lost child. A scavenger, just like them. Have you heard of a young girl going missing from around here?'

The old woman shook her head, dislodging a cloud of coal dust. 'Won't be nobody caring tuppence for a lost mudlark. This city has no 'eart for them like that. If you've got no coin, London just grinds you up into paste. Spits you in the gutter like rotten offal. I was a lady's maid once; would you believe it? In a fine 'ouse, too. Then me 'usband died and me looks and teeth fell away, and I was out on the street. London don't give a fig whether I live or die. It don't give a fig about your mudlark, neither. Best give up looking.'

And with that, she curled back up into her sacking, almost vanishing from sight.

'Well,' said Pyewacket. 'That was helpful, wasn't it?'

'Any luck?' Gigantus strode over, leaving the terrified bargeman to scurry away into the mist. He looked as frustrated as Sheba.

'Nothing,' said Mama Rat. 'How about you?'

'Another petty criminal who doesn't actually know anything,' he said. 'If we were looking for stolen silverware we'd have hit the jackpot twenty times over by now.'

Beside Sheba, Pyewacket peeped out from under his peaked cap. 'Letting that lumpy brute ask all the questions isn't getting us anywhere,' he said.

'I suppose you have a better idea?' Gigantus replied through gritted teeth.

'I have, as it happens. Didn't Mama Rat used to know some bloke round this way? Fat Albert, or something? Why don't we go and ask him?'

'You might be on to something there, dearie,' said Mama Rat, thoughtfully. 'It was Large 'Arry I used to be acquainted with. I remember he still owes me a favour or two.'

'What are we waiting for, then?' Pyewacket said.

'Nice thinking, Pye.' Sister Moon patted the top of his cap.

Pyewacket puffed out his chest. 'Yes, well. I'm not just a pretty face, am I?'

Sheba tried her best not to giggle.

*

The wharves were as crowded and chaotic as the Thames itself.

Piles of lopsided wooden warehouses leant against each other, stretching out into the river on rickety wooden stakes. Boats of every shape and size were crammed so tightly together, it seemed as though the smaller ones would burst into clouds of matchsticks at any second. A scribbly mess of ships' masts and wooden cranes blocked the sky, and rope was everywhere in twists and loops, tying it all up like a giant spider's web.

In between were hordes of bustling, shouting people. They were loading and unloading ships, hauling crates and boxes in and out of warehouses, on and off carts and barrows. It looked like chaos, but everyone seemed to know what they were doing.

The troupe edged along the dockside, dodging swinging bales of cotton and sweaty rivermen, all the time following Mama Rat and her cloud of pipe smoke. She didn't stop until she came to a grand wooden warehouse with the words 'Pickle Herring Wharf' painted across the front. There she stood for a few minutes, scanning the faces of the scurrying workers. Just when Sheba was beginning to think she wouldn't spot whoever she was looking for, Mama Rat clapped her hands together and laughed. She walked briskly over to a stack of crates and coiled rope where a man was sitting, whittling away at a hunk of wood with a pocket knife.

He looked up, and for a moment his brows rose in surprise. He quickly pulled them back into a frown, but not before getting a good look at the rest of them.

'You 'ave fallen in with a strange lot,' he said.

'Nothing wrong with being a bit strange, dearie,' said Mama Rat. 'Everyone, meet Large 'Arry. A very old friend of mine.'

'Friends, is it?' said 'Arry. 'I 'aven't seen 'ide nor 'air of you for years. I've got customers in

Mozambique what are better friends than you.'

'Now, now, 'Arry.' Mama Rat looked hurt. 'Don't be like that.'

Sheba stared at the man from beneath her hood. He certainly was large, although not compared to the solid bulk of Gigantus. Most of 'Arry's size was around his belly, which strained to burst out of his waistcoat. He had shaggy grey hair and a grizzled beard, stained yellow around his mouth from tobacco smoke. A typical sea captain, like a picture from a story book. He carved off a few more slivers of wood, before Mama Rat's exaggerated pout made him mellow.

'All right, then,' he said. 'What is it brings you and your motley crew down on the docks? After something, I don't doubt.'

'Just some information,' said Mama Rat. 'About a mudlark girl who's gone missing from the river.'

'One of those poor scraps what go rooting about in the filthy scum between the jetties, you mean? I 'aven't 'eard nothing about that, but then . . .' He paused. 'What's this information worth, exactly?'

'It's worth you keeping your face the right shape,'

said Gigantus, knuckles cracking. He appeared to be tired of waiting.

'Stop that,' said Mama Rat. 'I told you, 'Arry's an old friend. There's no need to scare him.'

'And I been threatened by worse than the likes of you,' 'Arry added. Even so, his hands seemed to shake a little as he went back to his whittling.

'Please, Mr Large,' Sheba said. She didn't want to draw attention to herself, but she was desperate to find out what he knew. 'The girl that's missing is my friend. I have to find out what happened to her. Anything you tell us will help, I'm certain.'

'Arry looked up from his piece of wood, into Sheba's pleading amber eyes. If he noticed the fur on her face, he didn't show it. The frown lines on his brow softened.

'I 'ad a daughter meself, once,' he said. 'About your age. She went missing too. Fell off a jetty and drowned.' He sighed and tucked his knife away.

'There was something a few days ago. Not about a girl, but still . . . I was unloading down on St Saviour's dock, when some of the lads started talking rubbish about noises in the fog, and children going missing at low tide. Now, I don't 'old with all that talk about monsters in the river and suchlike, but I do believe that there was some of them mudlarks what went out and never came back. As far as I 'eard, anyway.'

'What happened to them?' asked Sheba.

Large 'Arry shrugged. 'What do you think? Sucked down in the mud, I should expect. Who would be so stupid as to go walking around out there? And if the clay didn't get them, there's plenty of other things that might. This city's full of evil, you know. Murderers, thieves, baby farmers chucking kiddies in the river, doctors chopping up grave-robbed bodies . . . tales you wouldn't believe. London ain't no kind of a place to be growing up in. Not if you're paupers like that lot.'

The old sailor pulled his knife out again and went back to his whittling, as if saying the meeting was over. Mama Rat thanked him, and he grunted in a way that might just have been friendly.

The troupe began to make their way through the maze of docks to London Bridge, Sheba trailing at the back. *Other children are missing too.* She rolled the thought around in her head like Till's little glass marble. If that was true, then what had they stumbled into? And where could Till be now?

None of them noticed the shadowy figure they passed, hidden in the shelter of a warehouse doorway. The light was dim there, faint enough to hide the broad shoulders bunched beneath a black greatcoat, and the tip of a military sword that poked out underneath. It even hid the wide leather patch that covered half of his face, but not the gleam of his one good eye as it glared, never leaving the silhouettes of the carnival troupe as they walked away from the docks, towards home.

CHAPTER SEVEN

In which Sheba gets a sniff of
London's criminal underworld.

At the show that night, Sheba nursed a secret hope Till might return, back to tell her she had run away from her life as a mudlark after all. But there was no sign. And thinking about her made it hard for Sheba to put on a proper performance. Her gaze kept drifting out of the window, away from the customers, who saw nothing but the loose, tumbling curls of her hair: everything wolfish hidden from sight.

'You'd better start making an effort,' Plumpscuttle warned her, 'or it's back to that dump on the seaside, missy.'

The next morning, she lay in bed long after the others had arisen, staring at the patches of damp, cracked plaster on the ceiling. Now she had something else to worry about.

This isn't helping, she finally said to herself. *I'm going to get up and try twice as hard to find Till today.*

In one determined movement, she sat up and threw back her tattered blanket. She was just about to pull on her pinafore and go downstairs, when she noticed a large, rectangular lump in Gigantus's giant mattress. She recalled the way the big man was always scribbling away in his journal. Was it a secret diary? Or a manual on how to smash someone into a pulp?

The voice in her head told her to leave it well alone. It was a bad idea to pry into anyone's secret books, but if you did it to a strongman over seven feet tall, you were asking for trouble. The kind of trouble that required stitches afterwards.

But the book-shaped bump seemed to cry out to her. Her fingertips itched at the thought of uncovering it. Maybe just a tiny peek, she thought, as she reached under the bedding . . .

It was indeed a book. A large, leather-bound one, much bigger than his journal. She picked it up and opened the heavy cover. On the first page, written in careful copperplate script, was: *The Thrilling Escapades of Agnes Throbbington by Gertrude Lacygusset.*

Agnes Throbbington? Gertrude Lacygusset? Sheba choked back a laugh. Could this be what the big man spent all his spare time working on? She opened the first page, listening all the while for footsteps on the stairs.

. . . Agnes could feel her tiny heart flutter away like a tiny fluttery thing. Across the crowded ballroom stood Jeremy Gristle, the local pig doctor and the champion of her dreams.

He looked over the dance floor with his manly, steel-grey eyes. His face was elegantly chiselled, his raven hair hung about his broad shoulders. He wore a waistcoat embroidered with silver flowers. That was quite manly, too.

All around Jeremy, farmers' daughters were draped in flouncy layers of every colour, but he cared not a fig for them. Ever since their eyes had met over the pigsty three days ago, Agnes knew all he could think about was her.

When Jeremy caught her eye, Agnes's breath stuck in her throat. Even from across the ballroom, it felt as though she was falling deep into his gaze: as if their very souls were bleeding into one great big squishy blob of true love . . .

Sheba was trying to resist the urge to be sick all over the parchment pages, when she heard a creak from the stair floorboards. Her heart pounding in her chest, she shoved the book back under the mattress and tried to look as though she was just getting up from her bed. After a few seconds, when Gigantus failed to burst into the room, she peeked down the stairs. They were completely empty.

You really shouldn't be so nosy, she told herself. But she couldn't help feeling a guilty tingle of delight at having snuffled out a secret.

*

The others were in the yard, discussing what course of action to take next.

'Maybe we should go back to the docks,' Sister Moon was saying. 'We could ask some more questions.'

'What's the point in that?' Gigantus paused in his exercises. Today he was lifting the back wheels of the wooden caravan up off the ground and down again. 'Nobody really knows anything. We'll just hear more claptrap about monsters eating children in the fog. Morning, Sheba.'

Sheba looked at Gigantus with new eyes, trying to imagine the enormous strongman as Gertrude Lacygusset, romantic novelist. The two sides just didn't match. *But you really shouldn't judge people by how they look*, she reminded herself. To cover up her confusion, she joined in the debate. 'But if others *have* been taken,' she said, 'then couldn't it all be connected?'

'Why would anyone want to kidnap a bunch of starving river rats?' Pyewacket was perched on the privy roof, trying to summon up a spirit or two. 'If you're going to nab children, you'd be best off taking ones that you can hold to ransom. For more than three rusty nails and an old apple core, that is.'

'True,' said Mama Rat. 'But what if you weren't after money? If you wanted children for something else, then the lowest of the low is where you'd start. After all, apart from us, who's even noticed they're gone?'

'Maybe one of them doctors has taken them to peel open and look inside. Or something worse. I heard a story once about a butcher who chopped people up and made them into pies. Maybe he's decided to make mudlark muffins instead.'

'That's my *friend* you're talking about, Pyewacket!' Sheba snapped, and was surprised to see him look ashamed.

The argument was interrupted by a fluttering of wings as something that almost resembled a bird dropped out of the sky and onto the fence. It sat there, blinking and attempting to coo.

'What on earth is that?' said Pyewacket, a look of disgust on his face.

'I think it might once have been a pigeon,' Sister Moon said.

It did have a beak, and some tatty things that might have been feathers, but it didn't look much like a bird to Sheba. Not unless it was some new London variety that nested at the bottom of a coal scuttle.

'Horrible things!' Pyewacket clapped his hands and tried to scare it away. 'Rats with wings, that's what they are!'

'Just be careful what you're saying,' warned Mama Rat.

'You leave that bird alone!' Gigantus strode over from the caravan and plucked the pigeon from the fence with one hand. Sheba thought he might crush the mangy thing like an eggshell, but instead he held it tenderly between his giant fingers as he carefully removed a piece of paper from its leg.

'I wouldn't touch that if I were you,' said Pyewacket. 'You'll catch something horrid.'

'What are you doing?' Sheba asked.

'It's a letter from an old acquaintance of mine,' he said. 'Sent by homing pigeon. I gave him this bird years ago. Never thought he'd actually use it.'

'Sneepsnood?' Mama Rat asked, and Gigantus nodded.

'He wants to see us today. Says it's urgent.'

Sheba noticed a wary glance pass between the two. Sister Moon also seemed to tense beside her.

'Who's Sneepsnood?' Sheba whispered.

'A man that Gigantus knows. I only saw him once, but I didn't trust him. Some kind of criminal, I think.'

'Well, we'd best oblige him then,' said Mama Rat.

*

Sneepsnood's Emporium of Lost Treasures was a tiny shop on Whitechapel High Street. The bay windows that faced the road were covered in thick grime. If you peered really closely, you could just about make out display shelves crammed with goods of all descriptions. There were old music boxes, keys of every size and shape, tin cans stuffed with rusty nails, kettles, buckets, scissors, knives, forks and bits of machinery that had fallen off various steamers and ended up in the river. It looked like a load of useless, unwanted junk – but that was its exact purpose.

The splintered, muck-spattered door was covered in peeling playbills and posters, and when they entered a bell gave a dismal tinkle. The inside of the shop was also a chaotic, cluttered mess. A range of dressers and tables, most with missing legs propped up by books and old bricks, filled all but the tiniest bit of floor space. Every shelf and surface was covered with more useless items, some of which had entirely dissolved into sad little mountains of rust. There was a thick coating of dust over everything, broken only by the winding trails of mouse footprints. The place smelled of must and neglect, with a strong hint of rodent.

At the sound of the bell, a man shuffled out from the back of the shop. He was tall and thin, and wore a suit that was three sizes too small. He looked like a cloth-wrapped beanpole. His thinning grey hair was plastered back from his scalp with lashings of pomade and a pair of wire spectacles perched on the end of his hooked nose.

'Ah, you got my message then,' he said.

'Good to see you again, Jeremiah,' said Gigantus. He carefully handed over the pigeon, which he had carried in the gentle cradle of his fingers all the way from Brick Lane. Sneepsnood grabbed it as if it were an old feather duster and rammed it, squawking, into a nearby cage. Gigantus's craggy face scowled. *I really am learning lots about him today*, thought Sheba, as she looked on from beneath her hood.

'Come round the back,' said Sneepsnood. 'We need to talk.'

They followed him towards a door at the rear, creating a series of clatters as Gigantus smashed against all the shelves. After much ducking, squeezing and dodging they stepped through into the back room.

It was full to the brim, just like the shop, but instead of metal junk, it was full of silverware. Spoons, ladles, bowls, plates, goblets and tureens; stacks of them on tables and benches all around the room. A wide hearth filled one wall, and a fire was roaring inside. A blackened crucible sat in the middle, tended by a scruffy young boy. Every now and then he fed another piece of silver into the pot and watched it slowly dissolve into the thick, glinting soup of molten metal. On the workbench next to him were piled twenty or more bars of solid silver.

He was melting down stolen goods into untraceable lumps. So Sister Moon was right about the man being a criminal.

'Now,' said Sneepsnood, turning to face them with a knowing smirk. 'Word comes to me you've been looking for someone down on the waterfront.'

Mama Rat raised an eyebrow. 'Word travels fast, Jeremiah. How did you get to hear of that?'

'There aren't many . . . ahem . . . *groups* like yours in the city.' Sneepsnood smiled, showing grey gums and yellow teeth. 'And you seem to have asked an awful lot of people. Caused quite a stir in the underworld, believe me. Folk thought the peelers had started some new kind of taskforce.'[xiii]

'Well, it's nothing to do with the police,' said Gigantus. 'We're just trying to find a missing girl, that's all.'

'I'm sure you are, I'm sure you are!' Sneepsnood flapped his bony hands and smiled even wider. 'Very honourable too, I must say. Most public-spirited of you.'

'But what has this got to do with you?' Mama Rat asked. Sheba could see she didn't trust the man.

'Well, nothing at first,' said Sneepsnood. 'Just an

interesting snippet, I thought. Nice to know what my old friends are up to.' He gave another of his unsettling smiles. 'But then, as you know, I have a range of clients, from all walks of life.'

'I know that very well, Jeremiah,' said Gigantus.

'Yes . . . and it so happens that one of my patrons, a very well-to-do lady who is also searching for someone – her lost son, I believe – has already asked me to keep an ear out for this kind of thing.'

'So you told her all about us,' said Gigantus. His voice was a few shades short of a growl.

'Well . . .' said Sneepsnood, 'I may have mentioned it. But only to help further your enquiries, of course.'

'Of course.'

'Anyway, this lady would like to meet with you, and asked if I would request your presence at Christ Church graveyard this very afternoon. At one o'clock, if you please.'

'Why the graveyard?' Sheba asked. In her curiosity she had forgotten herself, and now found she had drawn the unwelcome attention of Sneepsnood. Even his gaze was greasy, and it was all she could do to meet his eyes without shuddering.

'A well-known place in the public eye,' he said, in one long sneer. 'Just in case any funny business were to go on. Suggested it myself, in fact.'

'Very well,' said Mama Rat. 'We shall consider it. Thank you for passing on the message.'

'My deep and abiding pleasure,' said Sneepsnood. The man fawned and smiled a bit more as they left the tiny shop, and even followed them out into the street to wave goodbye. They waited until they were well out of his sight before pausing beside a coffee seller to discuss what had happened.

'By Mr Dickens's inky pen nibs, I'm glad to be out of there,' said Pyewacket. 'That bloke has more slime than a bucketful of slugs.'

'Well,' said Mama Rat. 'That was all a bit peculiar.'

'I know he and I go way back,' said Gigantus, 'but I wouldn't trust him as far as Sheba could throw him. I would have said as far as *I* can throw him, but that's probably all the way to Hyde Park.'

'But what do we do about this lady?' said Sister Moon.

There was much rubbing of chins, fur and heads before Sheba found the courage to speak up.

'I think we should go,' she said. 'If we're both searching, we might be able to help each other.'

'You're right,' said Mama Rat. 'But maybe not all of us. We don't want to give the poor woman nightmares.'

'You and Sheba should go,' said Sister Moon. 'You'll know what to ask, and Sheba might sniff something. She's very clever at that.'

Underneath her fur, Sheba blushed. She still wasn't used to compliments.

'Very well,' said Gigantus. 'But the rest of us will be nearby. Just in case.'

*

Christ Church, Spitalfields. Sheba mentally added another note to her scent map. *Spilt beer, roasted chestnuts and raw meat.* Unusual things for a church to smell of, but then she noticed the pub next door, and the meat market across the road. All things that probably weren't there when the church was first built.

The building itself was just around the corner from Brick Lane. Made from grimy white stone, with a three-tiered tower at the front, it was easily recognisable for miles around. Crumbling hovels clustered around it, almost as if they themselves were bowing down to worship.

'Fascinating places, churchyards, don't you think?' Mama Rat said, as she and Sheba walked round to the graveyard at the back. 'Until they built the new cemeteries, there was barely any room here for all the dead. The gravediggers used to chop their way down through all the arms and legs to fit the new ones in. There must be thousands and thousands of corpses under our feet right now.'

Sheba shivered.

They had expected it to be difficult to spot the lady, but she was the only person present, seated upon a stone bench among the mass of crooked gravestones. From a distance, it looked as though she was hidden in shadow, but as Sheba walked closer, it seemed she was dressed in darkness.

She wore very fine clothing, but every last stitch was black.[xiv] Her skirts were thick velvet, her bodice embroidered with the silhouettes of twining flowers. A shawl hung over her shoulders, a bonnet covered her pinned-up hair and a lace veil hid her face. She was an absence of light and colour, as if giant scissors had come along and snipped a woman-shaped hole out of the world. The only bits of skin visible were the tips of her fingers where they poked from the ends of her lace gloves.

As Mama Rat and Sheba wove their way through the gravestones, the lace veil twitched as the woman turned her head. Sheba found it unnerving to be watched without being able to see any eyes. *Although,* she thought, *a veil would be a good way to hide your face. If I had one, I could go anywhere, and no one would know I was at all different.*

'Good day,' said Mama Rat, as they reached the bench.

'Good day,' said the woman.

Sheba wondered if she should say 'good day' too, but generally children were expected to be silent unless spoken to. Instead she took a subtle sniff.

Besides the local aroma she had just noted, Sheba picked up several smells around the woman: house dust or mildew, a trace of lavender perfume, a waft of chemicals and the hint of something more subtle – a familiar odour that she just couldn't place, like a

name that danced on the tip of your tongue.

'Please, do sit down,' said the woman, breaking Sheba's thread of concentration.

Mama Rat sat beside her on the bench, leaving Sheba room to hop on the end.

'I take it you're the lady that Mr Sneepsnood has been representing,' she said.

'Indeed,' said the woman. 'My name is Mrs Crowley.' She spoke with a strange lisp. 'I understand you have been making enquiries about lost children?'

'May I ask what that has to do with you?' asked Mama Rat.

There was a long pause, as if the woman were reluctant to speak. Finally, she gave a soft sigh and said, 'I too am searching for a lost child. My son went missing some months ago. He was playing by the shoreline one morning and never returned. Which is why I contacted Mr Sneepsnood. And several other businessmen up and down the river besides. I thought they might have some news.'

'Surely you'd be better off speaking to the peel . . . I mean, the police?' Mama Rat said.

'Oh, I have tried,' Mrs Crowley replied. 'And

they have assured me repeatedly they are "looking into it". But I thought . . . if there was another in the same position, we could somehow join forces. Share notes. And to know someone else who felt as I do . . . it would help me so.'

'It's clear you fear the worst, if you've gone into mourning already.' Mama Rat gestured with her pipe at the black dress.

'Oh yes,' said Mrs Crowley. 'I know it might be too soon, that there still could be hope. But without my darling boy . . . It wouldn't feel right to go about dressed as normal. I'm sure you understand.'

Mama Rat lit a fresh pipe. 'We'd like to help, of course, but we've only just started looking into the matter ourselves.'

'I see. And is it your daughter that has gone missing? Or a son like mine perhaps?'

'Neither,' said Mama Rat. 'Never had any children myself. Oh, besides Sheba here, of course. No, we're looking into the matter on behalf of some friends.'

'Sheba . . .' For the first time, the veil turned towards her, and for an instant Sheba thought she saw the glint of an eye shining through the thick lace, as if the lady was examining her. Then the lady turned back to Mama Rat. 'May I ask who those friends are?'

'I'm afraid that's private,' said Mama Rat.

'Ah. I understand,' said Mrs Crowley. 'But perhaps you could let me know of anything you might discover?'

'Of course,' said Mama Rat.

'That would be wonderful.' Mrs Crowley clasped her hands as if satisfied, although without seeing her face it was hard to tell. Almost as an afterthought, she took a calling card from her pocket. She moved to give it to Mama Rat, then at the last moment reached past her and presented it to Sheba. 'I look forward to hearing some news. Soon, I hope.'

Sheba looked down at the embossed piece of pasteboard, printed in an expensive-looking copperplate font. 'Mrs N. Crowley, 17 Paradise Street, Bermondsey', it read. She folded it carefully in half and tucked it into her cape pocket.

With a nod of her shrouded head, the veiled lady rose and left the churchyard.

Sheba and Mama Rat stared after her.

'Well,' Mama Rat said eventually. 'It's not often

you meet someone stranger than us in this city.'

Before Sheba could reply, Gigantus, Sister Moon and Pyewacket came dashing around the corner of the church. They looked relieved when they saw the others sitting on the bench, and slowed their pace through the maze of headstones.

'Thank goodness you're all right,' said Sister Moon, panting for breath. 'We saw a strange man following you. He had a long black coat and a funny patch on his face.'

'Where?' Sheba said, looking around the churchyard. 'We didn't see anyone.'

'He was walking right behind you,' said Pyewacket. 'I'm surprised you didn't smell him with that bloodhound nose of yours.'

Sheba was surprised too. 'Probably just a passer-by,' she said, but felt annoyed with herself. Had she missed a clue?

'What did you find out?' Gigantus asked. All three of them were clearly itching to know.

'We'll tell you back at the house,' said Mama Rat, with an ominous look around her. 'Away from prying eyes and ears.'

Chapter Eight

*In which the creature from the mud
strikes again.*

Barnabas Bilge awoke to the nearby bells of
St Mary's striking three in the morning. The
chimes had woken him at exactly the same time
every day since his very first memory. *Years and
years of getting up in the middle of the night and I
still hate it*, he thought, as he wriggled out of the bed
he shared with his mother, father and three sisters.
He stepped over a few more children sleeping on the
floor, and went through into the kitchen.

He didn't have time to light a fire to make
breakfast; his mother would do that in an hour or so,

when she got his sisters up for work. Instead he took a scoop from the bucket of pump water on the table and slurped some of it, then splashed the rest over his face to wake himself up. It was a lurid brown colour and tasted rancid, but at least it didn't have anything disgusting floating in it today.

He peered at the piece of cracked mirror standing on the mantelpiece and saw a grubby young man with eyes that looked much too old for his face. He rubbed at the fluff on his cheeks, wondering when it would ever turn to whiskers so he could grow a nice pair of sideburns.[xv]

There was a pot of cold gruel hanging over the fire: the remains of last night's dinner. Judging by the little footprints all over the cauldron, the mice had been at it again. They'd kindly left a bit for the humans' breakfast. He swallowed a couple of gloopy spoonfuls, then headed out.

The fog was thick again this morning. On the banks, the mudlarks were back. Even tales of missing children and river monsters couldn't keep them away, for they had no choice. Pick from the mud or starve. If the Thames had been full of piranha fish they would still have been there, trying to snatch as much as they could before their legs were chewed through.

Barney prided himself on being the best picker on the south bank. He was slightly less scrawny than the rest, thanks to his success, and the others paused to give him respectful glances as he passed. He clutched a pole twice as tall as himself, and it was this that gave him his edge.

While the other mudlarks had nothing but their own bare feet with which to test for sinkholes and broken glass, Barney Bilge used his pole. He poked with it as he slurped through the thigh-deep slop, finding solid footings that could take him out further than any of the others. Every now and then he'd strike something under the surface that he could scoop out, too. He'd found such treasures as a crate of pickled eggs, a silver plate and four human skulls. By mudlark standards, he was a millionaire.

Low tide was early today, and Barney was pleased he wouldn't have to waste time waiting for it. Instead, he waded straight in, trying not to shiver as his bare toes slid into the chilled jelly of the mud.

Dip, dip, dip went his pole, as if he were some

peculiar wading bird. Every now and then he stopped, fished something out and tucked it in his sack. It wasn't long before he had a pipe, half a pair of spectacles and a leather boot.

The fog folded around him. Step, prod, step, prod. He was just beginning to wonder if his luck might be off today, when he struck something solid.

With a hunter's zeal, he thumped his pole down again. It struck a second time, with a clang. There was definitely something down there, and it was *big*.

He began shifting his pole forward, bringing it down hard again and again. *Thunk! Thunk! Thunk!* The thing was directly underneath him. It seemed to be around ten feet long. Hard as iron. He wormed one of his feet further into the mud to get a feel, and soon met a smooth surface, studded here and there with spikes or bolts. His toes followed the contours as he wondered what on earth it could be. There seemed to be several hard layers, or plates, on top of one another, which meant it probably wasn't a chest or crate. Almost at the end, he felt a length of pipe or tubing and then . . . it *moved* . . .

Barney froze as the movement came again. The

thing had juddered beneath his foot. He quickly looked around to see if any other mudlarks were nearby in case he needed help. That was when he noticed the bright red tentacle poking up from the mud beside him.

At first, he thought it might be a bizarre eel, but then he noticed a puff of steam escape from the end. Soon it was gushing hot smoke, just as the thing beneath him began to grind its way upwards.

One of the talents that had kept Barney alive so long on the river was his speed. Several times he had felt the mud try to suck him under, and he had managed to pull his feet free and scrabble out of danger. Now his reflexes kicked in again, and he flung himself off the back of whatever-it-was and began pelting his way back to shore.

Anyone who has ever tried to run through deep mud will tell you it is almost impossible. The quicker Barney tried to pull his feet out, the harder the riverbed sucked them back in. He soon fell on all fours and began a frantic scrambling that was part crawling, part swimming.

As he wriggled his way to the bank – panting and choking – there was a great roar from behind him. The thing had exploded out of the mud and was thrashing about on the surface. Barney could hear the clank and grind of metal, the hiss and chuff of a steam engine. When he chanced a quick look over his shoulder, he saw a giant, crablike beast with a glowing yellow eye. The red pipe poured smoke out into the foggy air, and two jagged claws waved about, snipping and snapping as they tried to grab his feet. In the glare from its enormous eyeball, Barney spotted a movement: a shadow of something inside the beast itself. The smudge of a human face, floating in the centre of the eye like a diseased pupil.

With a scream of terror, Barney doubled his efforts, slithering through the mud like a demented eel. Luckily for him, some of the other mudlarks saw him thrashing around and dashed to grab his hands. Just as the thing's claws clanged shut where his ankle had been, Barney was hauled out of the mud and onto the riverbank, where he lay panting and crying at the same time. The mudlarks looked out at the river, faces pale beneath the muck and dirt, as the fog closed in around the clawed creature and it slowly vanished from sight.

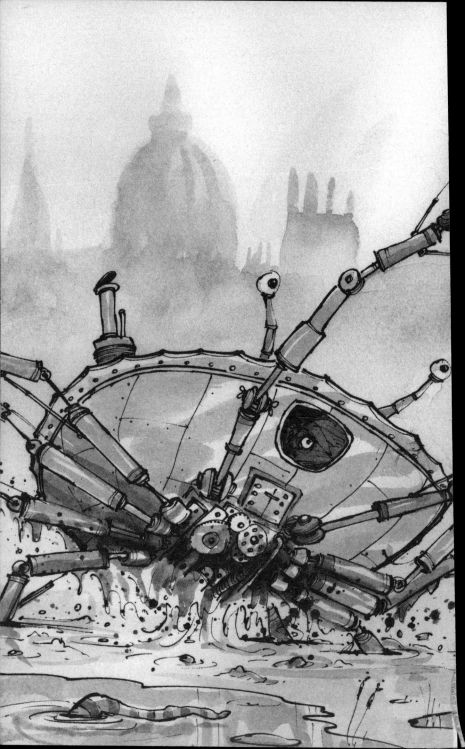

CHAPTER NINE

In which Pyewacket spies a vital clue.

The meeting with Mrs Crowley was still on Sheba's mind the next morning: the way her scent had been so familiar. A sense that everything was connected, but just outside of her sight. An invisible spider's web, and herself as a fly, about to blunder into it.

She mulled it over again and again as she sipped her coffee in the kitchen, until she began to annoy herself. To take her mind off it, she picked up Mama Rat's newspaper and found her eye caught on the headline.

WOUNDED COMPANY SOLDIERS DESERT IN LONDON

Reading it through, she learned that three soldiers from one of the East India Company's regiments had been shipped back from Bombay for some kind of treatment at the Warley Barracks.[xvi] All of them had disappeared soon after their ship docked in London. Running away from the army was a crime, it seemed. If the men were caught, they were to be shot by a firing squad.

More disappearances. Sheba swallowed her last mouthful of coffee and shook her head. Didn't anyone in London stay where they were supposed to?

What if the missing soldiers were lost in the same place as Till? she wondered. *What if they were taken for the same reason?*

'Now you're just being silly,' she said aloud, scolding herself. 'Not everything is linked, you know.'

Throwing the paper down, she headed out into the yard.

The others were already busy. Gigantus was limbering up for his morning's exercises. Sister Moon sat with her legs crossed, meditating again. Mama Rat had a saucepan of hot, soapy water, and was trying to coax her rats out of a hole by the kitchen door.

'You're not seriously going to give those wretched rodents a bath, are you?' Pyewacket called down from his perch on the fence.

'I am indeed,' said Mama Rat, over her shoulder. 'And if you say anything mean about it, you'll be next.'

'Not likely. My unique aroma is the source of all my magical power, you know.' The threat of clean water made him skip neatly along the fence, a safe distance away, before he gave a sudden yell. 'Visitors again! It's them mudlark folk back, and they've brought someone with them.'

Everyone except Mama Rat and Sister Moon dashed into the house. Sheba shut the back door behind her, then turned to peer through the keyhole.

There came a weak tapping at the gate, before it swung open to reveal Till's parents. They looked more than ever like two lumps of mud that had somehow grown legs. Between them stood another mudlark, this one literally caked in dried clay and stinking like an open sewer. For a moment Sheba's heart leaped, thinking it might be Till, but on closer inspection she could see it was a boy. He clutched the splintered end of a long pole in one hand.

'Begging your pardon, but we 'as some information which we fink might be of use,' said Till's father, bobbing his head like a very humble woodpecker. 'You did say we was to call on you if that should be the case . . .'

'Of course, of course,' said Mama Rat. 'Come in, please.'

The three of them shuffled into the yard and shut the gate behind them. When they were safely inside, and with no means of immediate escape, Mama Rat beckoned to the others in the house.

'If you don't mind,' she said, 'I'd like my friends to hear this. They do look a bit unusual, but please don't be alarmed.'

The mudlarks stared as Sheba, Pyewacket and Gigantus came out of the kitchen and into the yard.

'We is . . . er . . . very honoured to make your acquaintance,' said the father mudlark at last, taking off his hat and holding it on his chest. Sheba beamed at him. Many other folk would have stared in horror, or perhaps let slip a swear word or two.

'Pleased to meet you, too,' said Sheba.

The mud-caked boy goggled at her, but Till's mother managed a kind smile.

'What do you have to tell us?' asked Sister Moon. The mudlarks blinked, as they tried to remember why they had come in the first place.

'If you please, our friend Barney 'ere 'as an incredible tale. A very important one, we believe. Only this very morning, 'e was nearly snaffled by a creature from under the mud.' The man nudged Barney with his elbow, dislodging several clumps of stinking muck from the boy's clothes. 'Go on, son, tell the ladies and gentlemen what 'appened.'

Barney took a deep breath, then opened his mouth to speak, making spidery cracks in the layer of dried mud that coated his face. He told them about the crablike-thing and how it had come up from the river bed to try and grab him; about his escape and how he had been dragged to Brick Lane as soon as the other mudlarks heard his story.

There was a long silence afterwards, as everyone

considered his terrifying tale.

'This thing that tried to get you,' asked Sheba, 'do you think it could have been a machine?'

'A machine, miss?' Barney stared at her as if she were mad. 'It weren't no machine. It was a monster. A giant, clanking crab, just like I told you. And there was an eye. A yellow eye, with an 'orrible face in it. It must have been some kind of demon, like what the street preachers go on about.'

'But it had pipes and steam. Monsters aren't driven by engines.'

'Leave it, Sheba,' said Pyewacket. 'I think he's drunk too much river mud. It's probably melted his brain.'

'Be quiet, you toxic guttersnipe,' said Gigantus, 'or I'll melt your brain. Pull it right out of your ears and fry it over the stove.'

'Do you reckon this thing is what took our little 'uns?' asked the woman. 'You don't think it's eaten them, do you? I can't bear to imagine it: my tiny Till gobbled up by a giant crab . . .'

'It can't have eaten them, on account of it being a machine, you stup— erk!' Pyewacket was cut off in mid-insult as Gigantus's meaty hand clamped over his mouth.

'I think it may well be what took the children,' said Mama Rat. 'And I'm sure they haven't been eaten. This could be an important lead. Thank you for bringing it to us. Now, perhaps you should get young Barney here a bath and a nice cup of tea.'

With much nodding and waving, the mudlarks backed out of the yard, just as the sound of the front door slamming signalled Plumpscuttle's return.

'Shut the gate, shut the gate!' hissed Mama Rat, but it was too late.

Plumpscuttle's head appeared at the kitchen window in time for him to see the last mudlark disappear.

'What's this?' he yelled. 'What's this?'

'Here we go,' Gigantus muttered.

They all turned sheepishly to face the house as Plumpscuttle stormed down the kitchen steps, his face growing steadily more purple.

'People in my yard again? Uninvited trespassers on my property? You bunch of walking monsters know that visitors are forbidden here, don't you? If people want to gawp at you, then I expect them to pay me for the privilege!'

He must have lost all his money again, thought Sheba. And now he wants to take it out on the rest of us.

'Now, now—' began Mama Rat, but their owner wasn't listening.

'Don't you tell me to calm down! You lot don't know which side your bread's buttered, that's the problem. You don't appreciate who feeds and houses you, who pays for your comforts. Without me, you'd all be out on the streets, begging for crusts and offal. But do I get any thanks? No! All I get are shoddy performances and flagrant breaking of my rules. No respect! No respect!'

'You'll be respecting my fist in a minute,' said Gigantus, under his breath. Mama Rat put a restraining hand on his arm.

'What's that?' Plumpscuttle screamed, sending a cascade of spittle into the air. 'Think I'm afraid of you, do you? You great lumpy oaf! You might be able to crush me like a ripe tomato, but if you do I'll have you thrown into the darkest cell in Newgate prison. And the rest of your 'orrible friends will be homeless. Don't think I can't find more freaks . . . and better ones too. Now get on with your chores, and do them silently. If one single sound wakes me up, you're all out of here!'

With a final glare, he turned and stamped back into the house.

'What a delightful fellow,' said Pyewacket, when he was sure Plumpscuttle had gone.

'One of these days . . .' Gigantus flexed his arms, and Sheba could hear the threads in his woollen jersey strain and pop.

'I know, dearie,' said Mama Rat. 'But for now, let's just keep the peace, shall we?'

'What about the monster crab?' Sheba asked. 'It definitely sounds like a machine.'

'It still doesn't explain why someone is taking the children,' said Sister Moon.

'No, but it could be *how* they're taking them. And if we could spot this crab and follow it . . .'

'Steady, Sheba,' said Mama Rat. 'Don't get too carried away. It might be a lead, that's true, but there's not a lot we can do about it at the moment. I suggest we lie low here for a few hours. At least until old grumpychops has gone to sleep properly.'

With a frustrated sigh, Sheba went to fetch the shovel and muck out Flossy.

*

Pyewacket waited until the others were all busy, then slipped off to his favourite perch on the roof, a peaceful spot next to the chimney stack. There was no way he was going to help shovel sheep dung or shampoo rats. He'd much rather sit up here. He was always more comfortable among the tiles than down on the cobbles, anyway.

The rooftops of London stretched out before him: a sea of chimney pots and steeples poking up through the blanket of greasy mist. His own little private world; a secret haven, away from staring, mocking eyes.

He reached into his trouser pocket and drew out the battered set of tarot cards that Plumpscuttle had given him for his fortune-telling act. The tight-fisted brute had snatched them from a pawn shop when he'd first read about 'Pyewacket' the imp in an old history book. The whole thing was just a gimmick to draw in the customers – *come and see a real-life witch's familiar! Get your palm read! Witness its dark powers!* – but Pyewacket wanted to take it seriously. He'd always fancied having a special talent. Something interesting about himself, other than looking like a living, breathing gargoyle.

The problem was, it wasn't even a proper tarot deck. Half of it was missing, or had been replaced with playing cards and pictures from cigarette packets. Pyewacket had even had a go at drawing some himself.

But he was sure, with practice, he could make it work. He shuffled the crumpled pieces of pasteboard and laid some out now, trying to find a meaning as he spread them on the tiles, his tongue sticking out between his crooked teeth as he concentrated.

The Empress, the Fool, the ace of spades, Queen Victoria and Mr Wobble.[xvii]

He stared, and stared some more, waiting for a meaning to appear. A vision of the future. A message from the universe. The winner of next year's Grand National . . .

Nothing.

His mind was as empty as a mudlark's dinner plate.

With a sigh, he packed the cards away and instead peered down from the rooftop at the throngs of people on Brick Lane below.

I might see a ghost, he thought. *A wandering spirit. A lost phantom.*

London had been around for donkey's years . . . the place must be full of them. And there was good money in being able to talk to the dead. Rich folks paid a small fortune for a chinwag with their lost ones: he had heard Plumpscuttle telling his nephew about it.

Squinting his yellow eyes, Pyewacket stared at the crowd, hoping for a glimpse of a ghostly shroud. Maybe some rattling chains or a headless horseman.

All he could see were the usual folk. The urchins, the hawkers and the balladeers. Organ grinders, with their hideous piped music and scrawny tamed monkeys; stilt-walkers and jugglers; and, worst of all, the prancing advertising men with their sandwich boards.

Pyewacket had a strong dislike of being told what to do – and what to buy. Especially when he didn't have any money. The men with their signs and placards irritated him, but the ones that drove him *really* wild were those idiots in the stupid papier-mâché outfits. He had seen grown men dressed as giant cheeses, colossal boots, massive top hats and even a humungous sausage. All the other pedestrians pointed at them, laughing and clapping, but Pyewacket knew what they were really up to. They were trying to put images in your head, so you went to their stupid shops and actually bought a cheese, a boot, a top hat or a sausage.

A slow grimace spread across his face. In the distance, just passing Chicksand Street, were not one, but two papier-mâché constructions.

The first one looked like a bottle of cough syrup and the thing behind . . . goodness only knew what that was meant to be. It was round and bright orange with a number of segmented, waving arms, just like a giant octopus. Only its limbs were moving by themselves, powered somehow from within the suit. And from its back jutted a pair of metal pipes, both of which were trickling steam.

Pyewacket's face went pale. All thoughts of spirit-talking and card-reading trickled out of his head, like sand through an egg timer. When he finally realised the importance of what he was looking at, he gave a startled cry and flung himself off the roof and into the street below.

*

Sheba was just heaving the last of Flossy's dirty hay into the barrow, trying to avoid the little lamb (now back to his gambolling self) as he playfully butted her with both heads, when the yard gate began to rattle with a frantic beating. She dropped the shovel and spun round, while Gigantus and Sister Moon jumped into fighting stances. Moon had drawn one of her Bowie knives when the gate burst open, and the strangest creature toppled in.

The sight of it made Sheba and Mama Rat shriek, and even Gigantus jumped back in shock. It was a bright orange contraption with a man's head sticking out of the top and Pyewacket on the back, howling like a banshee.

'Help me!' cried the man. His eyes were bulging in terror. 'I'm being attacked! Get this thing off me!' He spun and whirled, trying to dislodge Pyewacket, and his suit's many arms flailed about the yard. Gigantus dodged. Sister Moon dropped and rolled out of the way. Mama Rat's saucepan of water got kicked over, and the rat she was bathing made a dash for freedom.

Finally, Gigantus stepped forward and grabbed hold of the suit. There was a crunching sound as the outfit crumpled, but at last the thing was still. The man inside looked as though he was about to either wet himself or be sick, if he hadn't in fact done them both already.

'Pyewacket, what do you think you're doing?' Mama Rat hissed. 'You're going to wake Plumpscuttle and get us all thrown out.'

'But look!' Pyewacket shouted. He was pointing to the arms of the suit, which were now feebly clicking and twitching as broken cogs and springs popped out of the joints.

'It's an octopus. We get it,' said Gigantus, unimpressed. He was still keeping tight hold of the man.

'It's not just an octopus. It's an octopus *machine*. It's got tubes with steam coming out, just like that boy said. Look! There's writing on the front.'

Beneath the queasy-looking face of the man, words had been painted in bold across the octopus's chest.

'Belinda Spindlecrank,' Sheba read out. 'Amazing Automata and Incredible Clockwork Creations. Bespoke designs a speciality. Workshop at St Saviour's Dock, Bermondsey.'

'Wasn't St Saviour's where Large 'Arry said the other mudlarks were snatched?' Mama Rat said.

They all looked at each other. Maybe, just maybe, Pyewacket had found them a clue. Sheba took a step closer to the octopus man.

'Do you work for this Spindlecrank?' she asked.

The man looked at Sheba and did a double take. He clearly thought he was trapped in some kind of nightmare. 'Yes, yes, I do,' he managed.

'And what kind of . . . *automata* . . . does she make?'

'What? I don't know! Clockwork things that move. Will you let me go and get this crazy brat off my head! He's got *claws*, you know. Like a demon!'

'I'll put a curse on you if you don't start talking,' Pyewacket whispered into the man's ear. 'I belong to a witch, you know. A *really* mean one.'

'Please,' said the man. 'Please. Just let me go. I'm only a sandwich-board man, I don't understand what you want from me.'

'We just want to know something,' Sheba continued. 'Something about your boss. These things she makes . . . have you ever seen one that's a crab? Steam-powered, like the suit you're wearing?'

'I don't know,' said the man, whining now. 'I can't remember . . .'

'Try harder,' said Gigantus. He gave the suit a squeeze and more cogs sprinkled out from the joints.

There were tears in the man's eyes. Sheba began to feel sorry for him, but still she had to know.

'I can't remember!' he said. 'There's a workshop, but I've never even been in. I just put on this suit and walk around in it. Now will you please let me go before I call for the police!'

'I don't think we're going to get much more out of him,' said Mama Rat.

'No,' agreed Sister Moon. 'And he's starting to cry.'

'Let him go, Gigantus.' Sheba stood aside as the big man dragged the octopus over to the gate and shoved it into the street, with a parting warning not to tell on them. He pulled the gate shut, just as a series of wet snorts came booming through Plumpscuttle's bedroom window.

They all huddled together and spoke in whispers.

'Well done, Pyewacket,' said Sister Moon. 'You found something important.'

'Yes, well spotted, dearie,' agreed Mama Rat.

'All in a day's work,' said Pyewacket, puffed up and pleased with himself.

'So, you think this Spindlecrank is the one what's been taking the children?' Gigantus whispered.

'Well, she's a machine maker with a talent for sea creatures,' said Sheba. 'There can't be many of those in London, can there?'

'So what we do now?' asked Sister Moon. 'Tell the police?'

'Not yet,' said Mama Rat. 'We need proper evidence. We'll have to get a look at this Spindlecrank's workshop.'

'Can we go now?' Sheba asked. 'We could be back by showtime.'

'Too risky,' said Gigantus. 'It'll have to wait until tomorrow. Just as long as that whimpering idiot in the octopus suit doesn't go and warn her we're coming. But I think he'll be spending the next few days hiding under his bed, after I described what I'd do to him.'

The others broke from the huddle and went to start preparing the house for that night's show. Sheba was left standing in the yard, still clutching the dirty shovel, almost tempted to rush off to St Saviour's Dock. Except, of course, she had no idea how to find it. *If you are there, Till, then you'll have to wait for tomorrow. Sorry.*

She just hoped that tomorrow wouldn't be too late.

CHAPTER TEN

In which our heroes battle undead creatures and evil engineers.

Sheba sat looking out from the bedroom window at the twinkling candles of Brick Lane. The fog was especially thick tonight, making them seem like will-o'-the-wisps as they shimmered and flickered in bright haloes all around.

From the room behind her came the rumbling of snores. Gigantus and Mama Rat were fast asleep and, judging by the wheezy squeaking sounds coming from the big box, the six rats were too. Sheba couldn't help giving a little shudder. Even Sister Moon was dead to the world, lying elegantly on her back, still wearing her smoke-lensed glasses.

Sheba was almost tempted to wake her up. There was no way she could sleep, what with everything running through her head, and she wanted someone to talk to. It made her think back to the long nights at Grunchgirdle's, with the sound of the sea washing back and forth below the floorboards. How she used to slip outside and watch the moon on the waves.

She decided to go and pay Flossy a visit. Sometimes she used to whisper her worries into his ears. All four of them.

Out in the yard it was dark. Clouds of mist blew across the sky, and she could hear distant shouts, cheers and even screams coming from the Whitechapel streets. Flossy was curled in a tired woolly ball, tucked up next to Raggety in the straw. If she hadn't known the horse was so ferocious, she might even have thought he was cuddling him.

Sheba sighed, and wiggled her cold toes on the damp earth. There would be no listening ears there, then. She was about to head back inside when she heard rustling from the direction of Pyewacket's cage. In the dim light, she could see him sitting up at one end, staring hard at his hands. Dreading what she might see, Sheba moved a little closer.

He was stitching something from scraps of material and coarse twine. A doll or figure, stuffed with straw from his cage.

Another step, and Sheba saw it was a man with eight arms: the octopus from earlier that afternoon.

'That's a very good likeness,' she said, making Pyewacket jump with fright and bang his head on the cage roof.

'Aaaaow!' he wailed. 'What are you doing out here, sneaking up on folk in the middle of the night?'

'I came to see Flossy,' Sheba explained. 'And then I was wondering what you were doing.'

Pyewacket glared at her, then went back to his sewing. 'It's a poppet,' he mumbled. 'I'm going to stick pins in it and put a hex on that octopus bloke. Stop him from telling his boss about us.'

Sheba couldn't help being curious. 'All this magic,' she asked. 'Is it real? I mean, do you actually have special powers?'

Pyewacket was silent for a few moments. Finally, he let out a deep sigh and tossed the poppet to one side of his cage.

'No,' he said. 'No, I don't. It's just part of the act. But I want it to be real. I would very much like to have something . . . something special about me.'

Sheba looked down at his oversized arms, at those strong fingers that let him climb buildings as quick as a whip. 'Aren't you special already?'

Pyewacket held his gangly hands up in front of his face. 'Not this. I don't want to be special for this. I want to show everyone I'm good at something. I want them to be amazed by what I can do, not what I am. You must understand. Don't you feel the same?'

Sheba thought about her own act. How she let the wolf slip from its leash when the crowds were staring at her. How she knew it would make them scream and swear and say horrid things – but better they were cruel about that wild, animal side of her than the real Sheba: the lonely little girl with the furry face. It was a mask, she supposed. One she used to impress and scare people. But it was also a suit of armour that protected the person within.

'Pyewacket.' She reached through the bars and took one of his giant hands in hers. The skin was soft and warm. 'You don't have to put on a show with me. I don't care if you can do magic or not. I just want to be your friend. The *real* Pyewacket's friend – not the pretend witch's imp.'

When he looked up at her, there were tears in his eyes, glinting in the moonlight. 'Nobody's ever wanted that before,' he whispered.

Sheba smiled. 'They do say there's a first time for everything.'

'Listen,' Pyewacket gave her hand a squeeze. 'I'm sorry if I was rude to you when we first met. And if I said mean things about your mudlark friend. I can't help it, you know. I just open my mouth and spite pours out. I can even hear myself doing it . . . but I can't seem to stop.'

'Don't worry. I understand.' And she did. It was easier to attack first, sometimes. Better to get a few shots in before the laughing and the name-calling started. If anything, she was surprised they weren't all like it.

Tiredness rolled over her then, like a wave. It had

been another long day. Sheba yawned and turned to go back indoors, but Pyewacket squeezed her hand again.

'Don't tell anyone,' he said, 'but my real name's Jack. You can call me that, if you like. When the others aren't around.'

'Jack.' Sheba smiled. 'Thank you. I will.'

They were interrupted by a flash of silver light as something streaked across the night sky, making Sheba jump.

'Nothing to be scared of,' said Pyewacket. 'Just one of the Perseid meteors. The sky's full of them this time of year. It means there's a conflict coming. You're going to have to stand up and face it – no running away.'

Conflict, Sheba wondered. Might that be something to do with Spindlecrank the puppeteer? *Worry about that tomorrow*, she told herself. Now was the time for sleep.

'Night night, Jack.' She let go of his hand and began to pad back to the house. 'You might actually be quite good at this fortune-telling business.'

'I just might,' he said, grinning.

As she stepped indoors, Sheba glanced over her shoulder and saw him lying back in his cage, watching the wide sky for meteors.

*

Not long after dawn the next morning, the troupe made their way down from London Bridge, past endless stacks of warehouses and taverns, until they reached a break in the solid mass of buildings.

It looked as if the riverbank had cracked open, creating a quiet little sidestream. A puddle of filthy brown water, from which a forest of wooden pilings jutted. On top of these, scores of wooden houses had been built, their upper storeys leaning out over the river, teetering on the verge of falling in. Sheba could see narrow wooden planks interlacing the structures, with figures balancing their way across like tightrope walkers.

'St Saviour's dock,' said Mama Rat. She pointed along the inlet to where brown water gurgled at its mouth. 'That there's the River Neckinger.[xviii] Flows into the Thames. And over there,' she gestured to the warren of rotten buildings, 'is Jacob's Island.'

'Cholera Island, more like,' said Pyewacket. 'You'd drop dead soon as you set foot on it.'

Sheba had no intention of going anywhere near it, and she was quite glad when Mama Rat led them around the corner to the Thames. Here were the usual clusters of boats, tied up to a series of rickety pontoons.

In the middle, looming over the other craft, was what might have been an old warship. Now it was a rotting hulk, stripped of its masts and rigging and left to slowly dissolve in the poisonous water. Faded letters on its stern read HMS *Swiftsure*,[xix] but in fresher paint was *Belinda Spindlecrank, Clockwork and Mechanical Automata Made to Your Precise Specifications. Enquire Within.* A wonky gangplank led up to a little wooden door, built into the clinkered side of the hull.

They hovered outside, cautiously eyeing two hulking figures that guarded the entrance – two giant wooden puppets. Bearded and dressed in chainmail and helmets, they seemed to be medieval warriors. One held a ball and chain, the other a shield and spear. The wood was bare, as if awaiting a coat of paint, and Sheba could see metal cogs and ratchets gleaming at the joints.

'Gog and Magog,' said Gigantus, sounding impressed.

'Who are they supposed to be?' Sheba asked.

'They're the guardians of London,' said Gigantus. 'It's an old legend, but they have puppets of them in the Lord Mayor's parade every year.'

'Powerful spirits,' said Pyewacket. 'Maybe this Spindlecrank is a witch.'

'Well,' said Gigantus, 'let's find out.' And with that he kicked the door so hard it burst off its hinges.

Mama Rat stayed outside to keep watch, and the rest of them made their way onto the ship.

Inside was a wide open space with benches lining the walls. The place was full of powerful aromas: metal, oil, wood shavings and varnish, and there were mechanical animals everywhere. Every available surface was covered with cogs, springs and sections of half-finished creations. Sheba saw foxes, birds, butterflies, crocodiles, lobsters and turtles. Some of them were so intricate and beautiful, she couldn't help but admire Spindlecrank's skill. But she didn't see anything that looked like a crab.

And then a heavy door at the far end of the room opened and, as if summoned, a tall woman stepped out. She was dressed in fashionable crinoline skirts, but was also wearing a waistcoat with countless pockets, each holding tools. Sheba spotted tiny pliers, tweezers, rolls of wire and spanners of all sizes. Her auburn hair was piled on top of her head and held in place by a collection of pencils and screwdrivers. She stared at them over a pair of half-moon spectacles.

'What is this?' she cried. 'Who are you, and what have you done to my door?'

'Where is it, puppet lady?' Gigantus demanded. 'Where's the machine?'

'What machine? My boat is full of machines!'

'The crab machine,' said Sheba. 'The one that's been snatching children from the river.'

The woman blinked at them for a moment. Her mouth opened and closed soundlessly, as if she was trying to think of something to say. Then she turned and dashed back into her private quarters, slamming the door behind her.

'Well, that's a guilty reaction if ever I saw one,' said Pyewacket.

'She must have the machine in there!' Sheba shouted.

'Shouldn't be a problem,' said Gigantus. He began to storm over to the doorway when there was the sound of a loud, metallic clank, followed by a grinding of gears.

'Be careful,' said Sister Moon. 'I think she's switched on a trap.'

Gigantus stopped. The troupe looked all around them, but the workshop seemed quiet and still. Until a trapdoor in the ceiling slammed open.

A scrabbling sound came from the open hatch – claws scraping against wood – and a chorus of ticking and clicking, like the inside of a pocket watch factory.

They all stepped backwards, holding their breath, waiting to see what would emerge. Puppets of some sort? Mechanical monsters? Miniature versions of the river crab?

A final clattering came from the hatch, and then a bundle of *things* came spilling out, dropping down from the ceiling to land on the floor. A mess of tails and fur and fingers, they writhed and wrestled for a few moments before separating into a group of hairy, wild creatures. Five monkeys. Real ones, made of flesh, bone and fangs.

Or were they?

The monkeys stared at them, eyes gleaming, teeth bared. Sheba sniffed the air.

'Something's wrong with them,' she said. She could smell their musky, simian scent, but that wasn't all. There was a strong chemical odour about them, mixed with hot metal, oil and . . . death. They stank of old meat, dunked in pickling vinegar when it was just on the verge of rotting.

Sheba moved away too, until her back was touching the wall. 'They're dead.' The words came out in a disgusted growl.

'Well, that one just winked at me,' said Pyewacket.

'Sheba's right.' Sister Moon had noticed the flaps of torn skin on some of the monkeys. They were dead meat, stitched over metal frames, stuffed full of brass cogs and ticking gears. Engine oil dribbled from the creatures' ears and noses. 'Spindlecrank has brought them back to life with her machinery.'

'Not for long,' said Gigantus. He made a snatch at the nearest one, then swore as it darted out of his way. As if that was a signal, the others scattered, scampering between everyone's legs before leaping to attack, claws and fangs bared.

Sheba screamed as one came straight at her face, quicker than she could blink. She had a glimpse of yellow teeth as long as her fingers, shooting towards her face. Then there was a crunching sound, and the monkey's mouth jerked sideways. Sheba turned her head to see the creature pinned against the ship's wall, one of Sister Moon's Bowie knives jutting from its chest.

Ticktickticktick went its workings as it scrabbled to free itself. Then the broken mechanism crunched to a halt and all signs of life vanished from the monkey. It hung there, truly dead, leaking oil and embalming fluid down the wooden wall.

'Keep behind me, Sheba!' Sister Moon had her second knife ready and was lashing out at the jabbering clockwork monkeys with her feet. Kicks that came quicker than lightning, knocking the monsters clear across the workshop.

'Someone has to get that door open before Spindlecrank escapes!' Gigantus shouted. He had grabbed one of the monkeys by its legs and was using it as a club to bat the others away. The thing flopped around in his fist like a dead fish, scattering cogs, nuts and bolts everywhere.

The memory of the cage door at Grunchgirdle's popped into Sheba's head. How she used to pick the lock every night for a temporary escape. 'I can do that!' she called out, reaching into her hair for a couple of pins. 'At least, I think I can.'

'Be quick,' said Sister Moon, slicing a monkey's tail off with her blade. 'I don't know how long I can hold them off.'

Sheba kneeled to the keyhole and slotted her pins inside. With her eyes closed and her tongue poking out, she began to feel around for the first lever that would let the deadbolt spring back. It clicked into place almost immediately, just as the sounds of crunching and screaming grew louder behind her.

'Help me!' Pyewacket was yelling. 'Get it off!'

'Don't worry, I think it just wants to give you a kiss,' said Gigantus. And then he began yelling himself as one of the monkeys clambered onto his head and began clawing at his eyes.

Sheba risked a quick look over her shoulder and saw Sister Moon throw her second knife. Her hands were too fast to spot: just a blur as the silver blade whistled through the air and knocked the clockwork monkey away from Gigantus. A few inches lower and it would have landed in the middle of his forehead.

Clunk. The second lever moved, and Sheba felt the bolt give a little.

'Nearly there!' she called.

'Just a couple of monkeys left,' said Sister Moon.

Peeking again, Sheba saw Gigantus peel one away from Pyewacket and break it apart against a rafter. The final creature somehow dodged past Sister Moon and began to streak across the workshop floor, heading straight for her. It was at that moment that Mama Rat stepped into sight, a flintlock pistol in one hand.

'What's going on in here?' she said, eyes popping wide as she saw the mechanical monkeys in pieces everywhere and the last survivor just about to spring at Sheba. Mama, calm as ice, drew a bead with her gun and fired, blowing the thing into chunks of meat and metal.

Sheba flinched, and with that movement the last lever clicked away.

The bolt shot back and the door to Spindlecrank's private quarters swung open.

'Oh no you don't!' A hand shot through the gap, grabbing Sheba's shoulder and shoving her backwards.

'Sheba!' cried Mama Rat.

Losing her balance, Sheba tumbled, but managed to twist in the air and land on all fours. She turned on the puppet maker, as full of hot anger as she had ever been. She saw the woman had pulled a strange-looking pistol from her jacket and was raising it to point at her, but she was too furious to be frightened. This horrid puppeteer had tried to hurt her friends, and could even have Till hidden away in her room. She deserved to be taught a lesson . . .

Sheba bared her sharp teeth in a snarl. Her fingernails squeezed themselves into curved claws. *I've never changed this much or so fast before*, she thought. *What happens if I can't change back?*

Behind her she heard a roar. It was Gigantus, stampeding towards the door. Spindlecrank switched aim to the lumbering giant and fired.

There was a twang, and Gigantus halted, slapping a hand to his neck as if he'd been stung. A tiny dart with bright red fletchings jutted between his fingers.

Spindlecrank frantically wound the mechanism on the side of the pistol, getting ready for another shot, just as Mama Rat was pouring powder into the muzzle of her pistol. But Sister Moon was quicker than both. She ran to one of the pinned monkeys, yanked her knife from the wall and flung it at the inventor, knocking the gun from her grip and sending it spinning across the floor towards Sheba.

Even as Spindlecrank made a grab for it, Sheba snatched it up and pointed it straight at her head.

'Don't move, or I'll shoot,' she said, her words coming out as a kind of snarl.

Spindlecrank put both hands in the air, 'Don't! It's loaded with poison!' she hissed, as the troupe surrounded her.

'What kind of poison?' Sheba asked. 'What have you done to our friend?'

Spindlecrank looked over to where Gigantus was still clasping his neck, swaying and looking very pale. 'I'm not entirely certain,' she said. 'A chemist mixed them up for me. Some paralyse, some cause violent illness. One makes boils burst out all over you. I'm sure he'll be fine, though.'

'I really don't think he will,' said Pyewacket.

And they all watched as the big man let out a groan and collapsed to the floor like a felled redwood.

*

While Mama Rat saw to Gigantus and Sister Moon tied up Spindlecrank, Sheba went to investigate the room where the inventor had been hiding.

Spindlecrank's quarters were quite different from the workshop outside. There was carpet on the floor, pictures on the walls, a small cot and a stove. There was also a drawing board by the window, and another workbench. Sheba saw several half-built clockwork bodies, waiting to be wrapped in flesh just like the monkeys that had attacked them.

There was no sign of anything crablike. No claws

or pincers, no rubber piping or steam engines. Had they made a mistake? But if they had, then why had she run away when they mentioned the crab – and tried to kill them with pistols and half-dead monkeys? *There must be something*, Sheba thought. She went over to the drawing board. Stacked upon it were sheet upon sheet of detailed drawings. It seemed that Spindlecrank carefully planned her every creation.

Sheba saw blueprints for everything in the main room, including Gog and Magog and the monkeys, and for others that either weren't here or had yet to be built. There was a tiger, a dragon, an elephant, tiny fairies and a monstrous snake. Leafing through them, Sheba was entranced. All the gears, all the mechanics. The way everything slotted together so perfectly, how the turning of the cogs and springs would make it all move, bring it to life. To the part of her brain that hummed and ticked like an engine, it was just like hearing beautiful music.

Lost in the magic of machinery, she was nearing the end of the pile when she saw it: the unmistakable shape of a serrated claw.

Laying the other sketches on the floor, she stretched out the broad sheet of paper and held it up to the light. The design showed a contraption with two colossal claws, a series of spindly legs and some kind of propeller to drive it through mud. There was also a porthole at the front, surrounded by tiny gaslights. It had a steam engine slotted into the rear, with pipes and vents jutting from under the carapace. And where its stomach should be was a chamber. 'Victim storage' was scrawled upon it.

'Found anything?' Mama Rat had poked her head around the door into the workshop and was looking at Sheba expectantly.

Sheba waved the plan at her. 'One child-snatching crab machine,' she said, her voice touched with a hint of growl.

Back in the workshop, Gigantus was still sitting with his head in his hands. Mama Rat had managed to pull out the dart, and now the big man was quietly groaning while Pyewacket patted him on the back. Sister Moon had the point of a Bowie knife at Spindlecrank's throat. 'What did you do to my work?' Spindlecrank managed to croak, raising herself on one elbow. 'You ruined my machines, you broke into my quarters! I shall call the police and have you all jailed!'

'Call the police, by all means,' said Mama Rat. 'And then maybe you could explain *this* to *them*.' She shoved the crab blueprint in her face, and Sheba noticed that the woman instantly began to tremble.

'That is nothing,' she said. 'Just a design. An idea. Drawing plans isn't illegal, you know.'

'That's funny,' said Sheba. 'Because a machine exactly like that one has been stealing children from the river.'

'That . . . that doesn't prove anything . . .' Spindlecrank stammered.

'Well, shall we turn it over to Scotland Yard and see what they make of it, then?' said Mama Rat. 'Or are you going to tell us exactly who you built it for?'

'I can't!' Spindlecrank cried. She was beginning to panic. 'I was paid to do it. They never gave me their names.'

'Not good enough,' said Sister Moon. She twirled her knife between her fingers, making it whistle through the air.

'There were two of them!' Spindlecrank wailed, spitting words out in a stream. 'One was small. He was skinny and sick-looking. He had a bald head and spectacles. The other was much bigger. I couldn't see his face, though. It was dark.'

'You must have more than that,' said Mama Rat. 'A banker's note, a calling card. Something.'

'I swear!' Spindlecrank pulled an oil-stained handkerchief from her waistcoat and began to sob into it. 'They contacted me by letter. There was no address. We met at night by the river, and they paid me in gold sovereigns. And . . . dead monkeys.'

Sheba and Sister Moon shared a disappointed look. Mama Rat nodded at them, and Sister Moon put her knife away.

'What will you do with me now?' Spindlecrank asked. Her whole body was trembling with fear.

'I have an idea,' said Gigantus. The big man had managed to get to his feet, but he looked almost as shaky as Spindlecrank. He wobbled across the workshop, reached down and hoisted up the puppeteer by her arm, until the two were face to face.

'You and I are going for a little walk together,' Gigantus said, growling, and marched her off the ship.

'I think we should be off too,' said Mama Rat. 'The peelers could well be on their way after all the racket we just made.'

Sheba nodded, and was following her out onto the street when she felt something heavy in the pocket of her cloak. She reached a furry hand inside and pulled out Spindlecrank's clockwork pistol. She must have tucked it in there and then forgotten about it. She thought about dropping it on the floor. After all, it wasn't really hers. But then again, it might prove useful in a tight spot.

Finders keepers, she thought, and slipped it back into her pocket before following the others.

CHAPTER ELEVEN

In which Sheba finds that even an innocent afternoon's entertainment isn't free of peril.

The next day, Sheba found herself moping around the kitchen, filled with heavy disappointment that Spindlecrank hadn't led them to Till. Whoever commissioned the crab must have known someone would come sniffing around the workshop. They had covered their tracks too well.

'It's not all bad,' said Sister Moon. 'We have a new clue, at least. The bald man with spectacles.'

'That's brilliant,' said Pyewacket, his head poking in the kitchen window. 'There's probably only ten thousand of them in London. We'll find the right one in no time.'

'Oh, be quiet,' said Sister Moon. 'Can't you see I'm trying to cheer her up?'

'Don't worry,' said Sheba. She went back to examining Spindlecrank's pistol. Losing herself in the neat arrangement of springs and cogs helped to take her mind off things.

She had the gun unscrewed and in pieces. Among the parts there was a circular spool of rings that held six shots. One chamber was empty, but the others still had small poisoned thorns in.

'Bet you can't put it back together again,' said Pyewacket.

'Bet I can,' said Sheba. With quick fingers, she slotted the pieces back in their places and tightened the screws with a miniature screwdriver from Plumpscuttle's toolbox. Then she wound the spring, cocked the hammer and aimed at Pyewacket's head.

'See?' She shared a laugh with Sister Moon as Pyewacket yelped and dived for cover.

It was just then that the door opened and a queasy-looking Gigantus staggered in. Sheba hid the pistol away, guessing he probably wouldn't want to be reminded of it. 'My head . . .' he groaned, slumping into a chair. His scarred face had a greenish tinge, and beads of sweat covered his brow.

'You poor thing,' said Mama Rat, fetching him a cloth. 'That nasty old puppet lady poisoned you good and proper.'

'I bet that poison would have killed a normal-sized man,' said Sister Moon.

'Thank goodness you're such a great lump,' said Mama Rat, mopping his forehead.

Gigantus moaned in agreement.

'What exactly did you do with Spindlecrank, by the way?' Sheba asked. She hoped it wasn't anything too horrid.

'I thought she might learn a lesson from some time spent with real monkeys,' muttered Gigantus, holding his head in his hands.

'Real monkeys?' Mama Rat said, in surprise. 'Did you cook something up with your friend at the zoo?'

'Perhaps,' Gigantus said. 'Let's just say that London Zoo's monkey house has a new exhibit today. Albert said he'd only keep her in for a few hours. Serves her right for shooting me with that stupid gun.'

Then he groaned again, and made a sound as though he was going to be sick. Sister Moon ran to get a bowl.

'Why don't you lot go out somewhere?' said Mama Rat, looking concerned. 'I think things here are about to turn a bit unpleasant. I'll send my ratties along with you. They'll keep you safe.'

'Right you are,' said Pyewacket, not needing to be told twice. He was out of the front door in a few seconds, and Sheba and Sister Moon followed close behind.

'We're best off out of there,' said Pyewacket, when they were safely on the street. 'Can you imagine that beefy gorilla being sick? It'd be like a tidal wave. We'd probably have drowned in half-chewed mutton.'

'Eww!' Sister Moon wagged a finger at him. 'Let's try and enjoy our afternoon without disgusting images, shall we? Where do you want to go?'

'We could visit the Great Exhibition?' suggested Sheba. 'You did say we would, and I'd love to see the Crystal Palace. And the giant diamond.'

'Too expensive, I'm afraid,' said Sister Moon,

looking at the handful of coins she had taken from her trouser pocket. 'We don't have three shillings.'

'What about the penny gaff down the road? They do an afternoon show most days,' Pyewacket said. 'We've got plenty enough for that, and some cake and lemonade besides.'

Sheba and Sister Moon agreed, and the three of them set off.

Sheba pulled her hood right down, and kept her hands tucked beneath her cloak. Pyewacket had put on his frayed old pea-coat and shoved his long arms deep into the pockets. His flat cap was pulled low over his face, hiding his yellow eyes. Apart from Sister Moon's dark glasses, they could just about pass for normal.

Through the door behind them, a nasty retching sound could be heard. Sheba trotted a bit faster, just in case Pyewacket was right and a giant wave of yuck was about to chase them down the street.

*

Back in Little Pilchton, Sheba had read about penny

gaffs in scraps of newspaper, which described them as seedy places, full of criminals and nasty people. They were actually cheap versions of the theatre, with a range of short acts that kept their rowdy audiences entertained for an hour or so. Of all the sights she had wanted to see in London, it wasn't top of her list.

'Aren't penny gaffs . . . a bit dodgy?' she asked.

'As dodgy as a seven-pound note,' Pyewacket grinned. 'Full of the lowest street scum, with manners like a pack of wild animals. And that's just the performers.'

Sheba shuddered, wondering if it was too late to head back and take her chances with Gigantus's wonky tummy.

'Where are the rats?' Sister Moon asked. 'I can't see them.'

Sheba sniffed the air. The scent of rodent was everywhere, but then there were probably more rats in London than people.

'I think we've lost them,' she said.

'Good,' said Pyewacket. 'Them things give me the creeps.'

They made their way along Cable Street, then turned onto the Ratcliff Highway.[xx] It was a tumbledown, dirty place, with people lying in the gutter and hordes of ragged children leaping around piles of rotting litter. The smell of disease and decay made Sheba feel sick, and she took her handkerchief out and held it to her nose.

Rot, death and squalor, she added to her scent map. *The place where everything unwanted in London washes up.*

'Lovely here, don't you think?' said Pyewacket, grimacing. 'The place is crackling with evil energy. I bet there's ghouls and lost spirits crawling all over it.'

'We're here,' said Sister Moon. She had stopped by a tall red-brick building that looked as though it might be an inn. The outside was covered with layers of playbills, ink faded into blurs by the weather. On the battered wooden signboards above the broken windows was painted the name: *The Old Rose*.

'I'll warn you now,' said Pyewacket. 'You might want to go and stick pins in your eyes instead. It'd be far more entertaining. The best bit will be the grub at half time.'

'Really?' Sheba hung back, but felt Sister Moon's hand on her shoulder.

'He's exaggerating,' she said. 'We'll have a laugh. Come on.'

'If you say so,' said Sheba. With Sister Moon beside her, she felt brave enough to go anywhere.

They stepped through into a small, crowded tavern. Sheba could smell lots of unwashed bodies, pipe smoke and gin, and also something sweet. Over in the corner she saw a makeshift bar, where a woman was selling apples and slices of unhealthy-looking cake.

A doorway at the back was open, manned by a scary doorkeeper. He was beckoning in the tail end of a queue, which meant the show was just about to start. They pushed through the unwashed bodies towards him and Sister Moon dropped three pennies into his hand. With a nod, he let them through into the theatre.

It was dark inside. Stuffy, hot and even smellier than the tavern.

At one end was a small stage, with space for three musicians in front. Then came a pit filled with scruffy boys in torn clothes, faces smeared thick with grime. They drank gin from bottles and chewed on apples, all the while shouting at the top of their voices.

Sheba and the others made their way to the back, where several rows of benches had been hammered together from splintered planks. By the smell of them, they had been fished out of the river quite recently.

Sister Moon grabbed hold of a rickety ladder and scampered right to the top, where she found an empty bench. Pyewacket followed, just as agile, but Sheba wasn't half as confident.

She clutched the splintered rungs, praying she wouldn't fall onto the heads of the crowd beneath, until she felt Sister Moon's hands around her wrists, lifting her up. Stress had made her claws come out, and she left ragged gouge marks in the wood. Luckily the place was too dark for anyone to notice.

From the top row they had a bird's-eye view of the whole theatre. The stage was badly lit, the view blocked by scores of fighting, shouting bodies. But at least the air was clearer up here, away from all the dirty clothes and festering armpits.

A few minutes later, a man in a tartan suit came out onto the stage, bowing and waving. There was an immediate roar from the audience, which made it impossible to hear what he was saying. It sounded as if he was boasting of the marvels of his show – a bit like Plumpscuttle did every night before their own performances.

The more the man went on, the more the crowd jeered. At one point, Sheba heard him say his theatre was as marvellous as the Great Exhibition, which made the whole audience fall about laughing. He seemed to take that as the final straw, and disappeared through the curtains at the back.

There was a brief moment of silence from the crowd, then a lady in an extraordinary amount of petticoats came on. There were wolf whistles and cheers, some rather pleasant music started – played by three men at the foot of the stage – and she began to dance.

She swayed from side to side, waving her skirts this way and that.

'Show us yer ankles!'[xxi] shouted someone in the audience, which was followed by lots of similar comments. The poor lady blushed crimson enough that Sheba could see it from the back row. She was so embarrassed that she stumbled on several of her twirls, which made the boys in the pit start throwing apple cores at her. One hit her on the nose, and she ran off the stage in tears.

'She lasted longer than most do!' Pyewacket shouted in Sheba's ear. She began to think that being in a sideshow was not such a bad job after all.

Before the curtain had even finished twitching, the man in the tartan suit was back on.

'Ladies and gentlefolk, may I now present to you: the scientific genius, Mr Faraday!'[xxii]

The audience shrieked and whooped as a man in a black suit and an enormous wig of wild grey hair came on. He carried a badly painted box, covered with coiled copper wires and strange dials and with a crank handle on the side, which he placed on a small table and pretended to tinker with.

'What's a scientific genius doing in a place like this?' Sheba shouted to Sister Moon, trying to make herself heard over the noise.

'It's not really him,' Sister Moon yelled back.

'It's just an actor. He's famous because of his new invention.'

Sheba remembered reading about it in the article describing the Great Exhibition. The man had built some kind of engine, hadn't he?

Up on the stage, the actor began to turn the handle, until his box exploded with a bang and 'Faraday' jittered about the stage as if being shocked, before collapsing in a smoking heap. The crowd threw more apple cores, forcing the man to scramble away on all fours.

When the interval came, Sheba was rather relieved. Pyewacket, along with most of the audience, went off to get some cake, leaving her to enjoy the peace and quiet for a moment.

'Is something the matter, Sheba?' asked Sister Moon. 'Don't you like the show?'

'It's all right, I suppose,' said Sheba. 'Not my sort of thing, really.'

'Yes. In Hong Kong we have musical theatre. You might call it opera. It's a lot more civilised than this.'

'Do you miss your home?' Sheba realised she had never even asked Sister Moon why she had left.

'A lot, yes.' Moon looked suddenly very sad.

'I'm sorry,' she said. 'I didn't mean to remind you.'

'Don't worry.' Sister Moon forced herself to smile. 'I'm used to it. One day I'll go back.'

'Why did you leave?' asked Sheba. 'If you don't mind me asking, that is . . .'

Sister Moon bit her lip, and Sheba could see she was wondering whether to tell her or not. She held her breath, hoping she would be found trustworthy.

'My mother,' Moon began, 'she's like me. With the eyes and the quick reflexes. Several in my family are. We all lived at the Tsing Shan monastery, where we trained in a Chinese fighting style called Wing Chun. Because of our abilities, we were very good at it. We were honoured for our differences, not locked away or put on show, like in this country.

'My father had travelled from England, wanting to learn Chinese secrets. Medicines, acupuncture, martial arts. Somehow, he convinced the Buddhist monks to let him study at the monastery. That was where he met my mother.

'When I was little, I thought they had fallen in love. But I think he just wanted to have a child with the same . . . unique skills . . . as her. As soon as I was old enough to have learned to fight, he stole me away and brought me here.'

Sheba's eyes were wide: twin spots of glowing amber in the dark theatre. 'Your father is in England?'

'Yes, in Newcastle.' Sister Moon shook her head. 'But he is a bad man, Sheba. He runs a gang of horrid criminals. So violent and scary. That was why he wanted to learn Wing Chun: to strike fear into his enemies. To cause pain and harm. He wanted me to become his right hand, maybe take over from him one day. But I could never live that life. The things he does to people . . .'

'So you ran away.'

'Yes. To London. Except I didn't have a clue about this place. Pyewacket and Gigantus found me in Whitechapel, being attacked by a gang. Mama Rat persuaded Plumpscuttle to take me in, to make me part of the show. They made up my stage name, to keep me hidden, and helped me come up with an act that displayed my . . . skills. It's not the nicest life, but it's better than the one my father had planned for me.'

For a moment, Sheba didn't know what to say.

Finally, she took one of Sister Moon's hands in hers.

'You poor thing,' she said. 'Maybe one day you can go back to Hong Kong.'

Moon smiled. 'Perhaps you can come with me.'

Sheba felt hot tears prickle her eyes. 'I'd like that,' she said. 'I'd like that very much.'

And then Pyewacket returned with the cake, shattering the moment into grimy, soiled pieces.

'What's going on here?' he said. 'Heart to heart, is it? Has Moonie told you her sad story?'

'Be quiet, Pyewacket,' said Sheba. She didn't mean to be so harsh, but she felt guilty for Moon having to remember her difficult past.

'Wait till you hear my tale, then. It makes hers sound like a walk in the park.' Pyewacket finished his mouthful of cake and handed the rest around. Then he cleared his throat, as if about to launch into a performance of his own.

'It was a stormy night on the Cornish moors, two hundred-odd years ago. All of a sudden, a bolt of lightning comes down, striking an old black pillar of granite known as the Hell Stone. The thing cracked in two, and curled up inside was a small creature, hideous to behold. (That was me, in case you were wondering).

'None would go near it, except for the old woman who lived alone at the moor's edge. A wise woman, she was. Or witch, as most folks call 'em. She took me in and made me her familiar, teaching me the dark arts before I even knew how to walk. And then, one fateful day . . .'

'All right, all right, we've heard enough.' Sister Moon shook her head.

'We're your friends, Pye, not an audience.' Sheba smiled at him. 'You *can* tell us your real story.'

Pyewacket looked down at his feet. 'I know,' he said. 'But it's not very dramatic. I was born just around the corner, in Shoreditch. My mum and dad were ashamed of me. Kept me locked up in the cellar. And then, one day, my old man sold me to Plumpscuttle's carnival, for five shillings and a bottle of ale. I was his first act, you know.'

'Were you really?' Sheba asked.

'I was.' Pyewacket reached across and took her uneaten piece of cake, cramming it into his mouth in one go. Then he spoke through it, spraying crumbs like a fountain. 'He had a couple more after me: a boy with a tail and some bloke who said he was older than Julius Caesar. They didn't hang around for long, though. Then he found Mama Rat and Gigantus, straight off a boat from France, and the rest is history!'

Sheba wished she had a tale of her past to add, but everyone already knew about her sad life with Grunchgirdle in Little Pilchton. Apart from that, what was there to tell? A half-remembered marble house that might just be a dream. A wooden box with carved flowers that could have come from a junk shop. It didn't make for much of a history.

Not that it mattered, anyway. Before she could say anything the audience had started shrieking again. It was time for the main performance, which turned out to be the strange story of a man who kept escaping from prison by tying bedsheets together and picking locks. He wasn't even doing it right, Sheba noticed in disgust.

'What's all this about?' she asked, as the hero was being chased around the stage by an angry mob.

'Story of Jack Sheppard,' said Pyewacket, 'most

famous jailbreaker in the world. Robbed from the rich, broke the hearts of half the women in London and escaped from every lock-up they held him in. Nobody ever told *him* what to do. My hero.'

It was about as well acted as a Punch and Judy show, but the crowd seemed to love it. They whooped and cheered so loudly it made Sheba's ears ring.

Then it was all over. The roars began to subside and everyone suddenly stood up.

'We'd better go now,' Sister Moon said. 'The owner gets cross if you don't leave quickly. They want to make room for the next audience. To earn as much money as possible.'

Sheba noticed the tartan-suited man had returned, this time with a pair of very large henchmen. The rest of the crowd was heading for the door as fast as the crush allowed.

With Sister Moon helping, Sheba scrambled down the ladder as quickly as she could. The three of them plunged into the throng and, holding hands tightly, were somehow swept along, through the door and into the street outside.

*

'Heavens above,' said Sheba, as she rearranged her cloak. 'Isn't there a better way of getting out of the place?'

One of the unspoken laws of London was that, as soon as three or more people stood still for a minute, a horde of street vendors and ballad singers would descend on them like a swarm of flies on a fresh pile of manure. The crowd that had previously been the audience now filled the street and, as if a secret signal had gone out, they were suddenly set upon by jugglers, cardsharps and pie sellers, all trying to squeeze some extra pennies out of them.

Sheba and the others dodged a mime, a clothes-peg hawker and an acrobat before they were finally cornered by a crusty old woman with filthy grey hair and no teeth. She shoved a basket of rotten pastries at them and screeched in a broken voice.

'Pork pie, luvvie? Pig in a blanket?'

Sheba stepped back from the reeking meat, just as a gang of small children bustled past. Pyewacket instantly hopped in front of her and shouted over his shoulder, 'Watch your pockets! They're dippers, and she's their kidsman!'

Sheba wondered for a moment what language he was speaking, and then realised he was talking about the children picking her pockets. She was about to tell him she had nothing worth taking, when she remembered the clockwork pistol and Till's marble. Her hands flew to the pouches in her cloak lining. Thankfully, everything was still there. The hideous old pie woman screeched something rude at them and spat on the cobbles.

'Watch who you're gobbing at!' Pyewacket shouted after her. 'I'll put a curse on you! A really disgusting one!'

Sister Moon looked at the crowd around them, frowning. 'This isn't a good place,' she said. 'We'd better go before there's trouble.'

Sheba agreed. Time was getting on, and this wasn't the spot to spend a pleasant evening. Not unless you enjoyed getting robbed, murdered and maybe robbed again.

She was about to follow the others back to Brick Lane when something in a doorway across the road caught her eye. Her feet became rooted, hair bristled all over her body.

'Sheba, we'd better go,' Sister Moon repeated, grabbing hold of her arm. Then she noticed the look on Sheba's face. 'What is it?'

'Over there,' Sheba whispered. 'In the doorway.'

There were several figures lounging on the pavement and against the wall, every one of them looking like they would happily slit your throat for tuppence. But one of them in particular stood out.

Tall, broad and wearing a long black coat, he had a leather patch that covered the whole left side of his face.

'The man from the graveyard!' Sister Moon clutched Sheba's arm. 'The one that was following you! That's him!'

Luckily, he hadn't noticed them. He was deep in conversation with three other men. All had wounds of some kind – an eyepatch, an arm in a sling and a bandaged head – and they shared the same brown skin.

'Lascars,' said Sister Moon. 'They crew ships from India, and lodge around these parts while they're in dock.'

Sheba remembered the article from Mama Rat's paper. Three wounded soldiers from the East India Company who had deserted. Could they possibly be the same men?

There was only one thing she could do.

'I'm going to get closer,' she said. 'I have to hear what they're saying.'

'Sheba, it's far too dangerous!' Sister Moon tried to pull her away, but Sheba's mind was made up. Even though her whole body had started to tremble with fear.

Pyewacket, having walked twenty yards down the road before realising the others weren't with him, scampered back. 'What's the hold-up?' he said. 'We should be hooking it out of here, not standing around taking the air.'

'Stay here,' Sheba said and, before Sister Moon could stop her, she pulled her hood down hard and headed towards the men.

This is the most idiotic thing you've ever done, she told herself, as she weaved her way through the milling crowd. But she knew in her bones that this was it – her chance. If she didn't do something now, then Till would slip away from her. She would never spot the patched man again, not among the teeming hordes of London. Besides, Sister Moon and Pyewacket were with her. If there was any trouble they would save her . . . wouldn't they?

The people around were all too busy talking, laughing and drinking to notice her. She made it to the building opposite in no time and pressed herself up against the wall.

Ignoring the clumps of soot and grime that smeared her cape, Sheba slid along to the doorway and then crouched down, trying her hardest to look like a homeless orphan, snatching a few moments of sleep.

Just to her left, mere inches away, the four men were talking in hushed voices. But not quiet enough to escape Sheba's wolflike hearing.

'It is time,' one was saying, his voice deep and commanding. 'You have hidden here long enough. I will take you to the house, and you can help us with the task.'

There were words of agreement and relief from two of the men, but the third sounded less sure.

'But, Major . . .'

'What? Do you have a problem with your mission? Are you not grateful that I've brought you here?'

There was a long pause. Finally, the man spoke, his voice shaking slightly. 'It's not that, Major. It's just that what you ask . . .'

A thump. The scared man had been shoved against the wall. 'You're squeamish? Really? After everything this country has taken from you . . . after they have stolen our homes, crushed our people, made us fight and die for them. After they have left us all scarred like this . . . How can you not want to pay them back?'

'But to harm innocents,' said the scared man. 'That would make us just as bad. I can't . . . I won't do it.'

'Fine.' There was a scuffle, and Sheba saw the man with the wounded arm shoved out into the street.

'Go, then!' The patched man, the Major, was shouting. 'But you're on your own. They will find you and shoot you. And you will miss out on our reward.'

Sheba watched the scared man stumble off into the crowd. Then, among stares and murmurs, the

Major and the others headed off, walking swiftly down the Highway.

Sister Moon and Pyewacket ran over to her as she stood up, brushing black dust off her cape.

'We have to follow them,' Sheba said. *Innocents. Revenge.* Her gut told her these men had something to do with the missing mudlarks. She could almost smell it.

'Follow that lot?' Pyewacket goggled down the street after the strangers. 'You must be joking. They look like they'd pop our eyeballs out, just for a laugh.'

'I'm not sure about this, Sheba. Not on our own—'

But before Sister Moon could finish, Sheba was off through the crowd, chasing the scent of the Major like a two-legged bloodhound. Pyewacket and Sister Moon shared a stricken glance before dashing after her.

They happened to have forgotten all about their ratty escort. It was lucky that Mama Rat's darlings, scuttling along the gutters and rooftops after them, had better memories.

CHAPTER TWELVE

In which Sheba has a brush with death.

They followed the three men along the Highway, past St Katharine's Docks and out of the East End. All the while they kept as far behind as they could without losing sight of them. Every now and then, Sister Moon would push them into a doorway or behind a hawker's street stall. Split seconds later, one of the men would turn and glare back up the road, but see nothing. *It's almost as if she knows when they are about to look round*, Sheba thought. Perhaps her reflexes were so fast, she could react to the slightest twitch of her quarry.

They walked past the piece of old wall that

marked the edge of Roman Londinium, then alongside the Tower of London. Sheba shivered as she passed it, imagining swirls in the mist were the ghosts of beheaded prisoners watching them. The spirit of Anne Boleyn, maybe.[xxiii] Or poor Lady Jane Grey.[xxiv]

They walked over London Bridge, which was crowded with hansom cabs, carts and horses, and scores of people in between, hurrying to get away from the stink of the Thames.

Once over the river, they headed down Tooley Street, holding their breath for as long as they could past the tanning yards. Once or twice they lost sight of the three men in the crowds, but Sheba still had a hold of the Major's scent. She followed it as if it were an invisible rope, a secret trail only she could trace.

It led them through a maze of streets, past docks and warehouses and onto a wide, cobbled road that looked as if it might once have been a grand place to live. On either side stood three-storey stone houses with high, square windows and tall chimney stacks. Most had steps up to the front doors. But all the painted wood was peeling, the sagging roofs were shedding slates like autumn leaves, and the windows were cracked and filthy.

'If we're not back soon, Plumpscuttle is going to skin us alive,' said Pyewacket.

'Quiet,' hissed Sister Moon. 'They're stopping.'

The three of them ducked into a nearby doorway and watched as the Major walked up the stone steps of one house and pulled on the bell. There was a moment's pause before the door opened and a stooped man stepped out. He had scrawny limbs and an oversized head. White frizz jutted out around his ears, but there was no hair anywhere else on the bulging dome of his skull. He also wore a pair of thick, metal-rimmed glasses.

Sheba clutched Pyewacket's arm. 'Remember what Spindlecrank said about the man who paid for the crab?'

'Skinny,' said Pyewacket.

'Bald,' said Sister Moon.

'And spectacles,' added Sheba. 'Exactly.'

The Major gestured to the two wounded men, who shook hands with the bald one, then all four walked inside the house. As the slam of the door echoed down the street, Sheba and the others stepped out of their hiding place.

'That's it,' she said. 'We've found them. They must be the ones who've taken Till. She could even be inside that house right now.'

'Number seventeen,' Sister Moon said, peering down the street at the house. 'We should go back and tell Mama Rat. She'll know what to do.'

Something about the number made Sheba pause. She looked around the road for a street sign, finally spotting one screwed to the side of a building behind them. *Paradise Street*.

'What is it, Sheba?' asked Pyewacket. 'You look like someone's just walked over your grave.'

'Seventeen, Paradise Street,' Sheba replied. She drew out the pasteboard calling card from her cloak pocket and unfolded it.

The house was Mrs Crowley's.

'She knows them! What's the chance of that?' Pyewacket's face boggled and bulged as he became more outraged. 'She was stringing us along from the start!'

Sheba frowned. The scruffy house didn't seem to

fit with the fine clothes Mrs Crowley wore, nor her posh accent. It seemed that it was all connected – could it be just a coincidence? Somewhere, a ship's horn sounded. The river where Mrs Crowley's son had supposedly gone missing wasn't far. Could she have been telling the truth about him disappearing from the riverbank?

'They might be helping her look for her son,' Sheba suggested. 'There might be an innocent explanation.'

'I doubt it,' said Pyewacket. 'I *know* this involves the missing nippers. I can sense it with my third eye.'

Sister Moon looked as puzzled as Sheba. 'Maybe they've captured Mrs Crowley, too? Or they've come to ask her for a ransom?'

Pyewacket shook his head. 'No chance. They've got the mudlarks tied up in the basement somewhere and they're about to eat them for supper.'

Beneath her hood, Sheba's jaw clenched. 'There's only one way to find out.'

'What are you thinking, Sheba?' Sister Moon asked. 'That we break into the house?'

Sheba nodded, and Pyewacket let out a gasp of horror. 'You must be crazy,' he said. 'Anyway, we're supposed to be back at Brick Lane. Plumpscuttle will kill us if we're not in time for the show – unless that lot do it first.'

'We'll be quick,' said Sheba. 'If we don't discover anything about Till, we'll be out again and on our way home straight away.'

'But we're bound to get caught,' Pyewacket whined. 'Caught and thrown in a dungeon somewhere.'

'We might be all right,' said Sister Moon, rubbing her chin. 'It's not the first house I've sneaked into. As long as you're both quiet as mice and do as I say.'

'We can get in round the back.' Sheba was already off, slinking down the street. The success of raiding Spindlecrank and spying on the Major had made her bold.

Pyewacket began to twitch even more. 'I've got one of my feelings about this. A bad one!' But the others were already heading off, behind the row of houses. He had no choice but to follow, grumbling all the way.

The three mismatched figures scurried down the alley. It was narrow and thick with shadows, with splintered fences close on both sides. Sister Moon stepped into the darkness, pulling off her glasses so her onyx eyes could see.

'Come on,' she whispered. 'In and out. As quick as we can.'

'In and out,' Sheba repeated, joining her.

Pyewacket stood for a moment on his own, dithering, before one of Sister Moon's arms reached out from the alley and yanked him in.

*

A few moments later, they were standing at the back door of number 17. Nobody had rushed out to seize them yet. The small garden around them was a mass of weeds and brambles, hiding them from sight.

Sheba heard a church clock strike six somewhere in the distance. They would have to be quick if they were to get back in time for the show at eight. But as she reached out with a trembling hand to try the handle, she found it was locked tight.

'Pick the lock,' Sister Moon whispered. 'Like you did at Spindlecrank's.'

Sheba pulled a couple of hairpins from her head and bent the ends with her teeth. She silently thanked

Grunchgirdle for locking her in that cage every night. If he hadn't, they would have been spending a lot of time stuck outside shut doors.

Her fingers worked quickly, but the thought of the Major being just behind the door made her breath catch in her throat. Her hand shook, rattling the pins against the lock. She forced herself to take some deep breaths and tried again. This time, the levers all clicked into place and the door swung slowly open.

They entered a dark and empty kitchen, silent and still. An unlit stove stood in the corner. Chipped plates were stacked on the table. It was an unnatural feeling, being in a house uninvited. Every bone in Sheba's body told her it was wrong, that she was trespassing where she shouldn't.

A door in the corner stood ajar, and a mumble of voices drifted through it. Two men, Sheba thought, in another room. Perhaps the wounded soldiers?

They tiptoed past the doorway and started up what would have been the servants' staircase. Sister Moon led the way, with Pyewacket clinging to her arm. Sheba followed, trying to put her feet exactly where Moon did. Every time the stairs made a tiny creak, her heart nearly stopped beating.

The whole place was dark, yet Sister Moon moved with confidence, as if it were broad daylight. *I wish I had eyes like that*, thought Sheba. Even with her own wolfish senses, she could only pick out dim outlines of the walls and stairs, but she could smell mildew, dust and woodworm. The sad scents of a place empty and forgotten. Mrs Crowley – if this was indeed her house at all – hadn't been living here very long.

When they got to the second floor, they stepped onto a wide landing in the main part of the house. It was lit only by flickering gaslight. The paper on the walls was yellowed with age and the floorboards were scuffed and warped. There were no grand paintings, no potted plants or ornaments. The place was bare. If it hadn't been for the dim murmur of voices in a room somewhere, she would have thought it derelict and abandoned.

They made their way down the landing to the source of the noise, stopping by a heavy oak door which gleamed with light at the cracks. There were voices inside – two or three people at least. Sheba looked at the others, wide-eyed. Her courage had now completely drained away, and she realised she was standing in a stranger's house, a few feet away from the owner herself and possibly some very nasty villains. She motioned back down the stairs, meaning: *I didn't really think this through. Perhaps we should go now?*

Sister Moon shook her head. She pointed to the keyhole and held her fingers to her eye in a circle. Then she pointed to Sheba.

Why me? Sheba mouthed, but it was obvious. She had the best hearing, and she might also be able to pick up a scent through the tiny hole. Sister Moon and Pyewacket edged back along the landing to where another door stood open. *Thanks a bunch*, Sheba thought, but she bent her head to the keyhole.

Although half the room was out of sight, she could make out a thick, musty rug, ornate chairs and a chipped sideboard with a tea service on top. On the walls hung two large oil portraits in ornate ebony frames. One was of a beautiful woman, dressed in cascading folds of white silk. The other showed a handsome army officer, hand on sword and with a backdrop of some faraway country. Both were blurred by a thick coating of dust. Mrs Crowley's ancestors, perhaps? Or the people who used to own this crumbling house?

Sheba almost didn't notice Mrs Crowley at first. The way she sat motionless in a high-backed leather armchair, covered from head to foot with layers of black cloth: she looked like a shrouded statue. It was only the tips of her fingers that gave her away. They twitched on the arm rests as she stared at the two figures before her.

One was the Major. His broad shoulders stretched out the fabric of his long coat. His shaved head gleamed in the lamplight, and that wide, leather patch hid the side of his face.

The other figure was the stooped, bald man. He wore a stained frock coat, fraying at the cuffs, and was clearly quite excited about something. He was waving his arms and hopping from foot to foot.

Sheba was now close enough to pick up their scents. The Major smelled of starch, boot polish and simmering anger. The stooped man reeked of chemicals. Pickling solution, like the puppeteer's monkeys. And there was a hint of something nasty beneath: rotten meat, dead things. Both odours set Sheba's hackles on edge. She felt an urge to turn and run back down the stairs but, somehow, she fought it. She had to stay and hear what they were saying.

'Are you sure you will be able to get it?' the bald man was asking. 'They have it very well guarded.'

'You just worry about your part,' came the lisping voice of Mrs Crowley. 'Leave the rest to me.'

'Yes, but without it, I will not be able to make it work—'

'Brother, dear.' Mrs Crowley leant forward in her chair. She sounded as though her patience was wearing thin. 'I have assured you that I will be able to obtain it.'

Sheba frowned at the keyhole. *Brother!* Then there was no question they were all in it together. But what was this thing they were after?

'Now, about the children . . .'

Sheba's heart began to beat so loudly, she thought they would be able to hear it on the other side of the door. She had to focus on calming herself so she could pay proper attention again.

'One more should be sufficient,' the brother

was saying. 'If only that last boy hadn't managed to escape.'

'But the tides aren't right tonight.' The Major's voice rumbled like a brewing thunderstorm. He had a slight accent, Sheba realised. And for some reason it seemed familiar.

'Very well, Major Kapoor. Tomorrow, then. At low tide – just as with the others. Within hours, we shall have what we most desire. And how long we have waited . . .'

That woman, Sheba thought. And to think she had felt sorry for her. There clearly was no lost son. And Mrs Crowley was no grieving mother.

'Yes, but something has happened to the puppet maker,' the brother said. 'And there's that bunch of misfits looking for one of the children—'

Sheba caught a strong waft of Mrs Crowley's scent as she jerked forward in her chair. 'The puppet maker owed money to some nasty people,' she snapped. 'Why do you think she was so keen to take our coin? They must have lost patience with her in the end. And as for those irritating snoops, they can easily be scared off. I met them, don't forget, and they were just as stupid as I expected. The woman was clueless, and as for that hideous little girl . . . my friend here has a cure for her.'

The Major gave a deep chuckle that sounded more like a lion growling. It was followed by the sound of sharp metal being drawn from a scabbard. Sheba caught a glimpse of a long steel sabre. A soldier's weapon that smelled of dried blood – human blood. Without meaning to, she let out a tiny squeak of terror.

'What was that?' came Mrs Crowley's sharp whisper.

Heavy footsteps began to approach the door. The iron-and-blood stink drew closer and closer. Sheba wanted desperately to run, but for some reason her feet were rooted to the floor.

The door handle began to move, she could see it from the corner of her eye, but still her legs were stuck like stone. *Run, you stupid girl. Run!* she shouted to herself. Where was the wolf when she really needed it?

Just as the door began to creak open, she felt a hand on her shoulder. She looked round.

It was Sister Moon.

Instantly, life returned to her limbs. Sheba scampered along the landing and into the room where Pyewacket was hiding.

Behind her, the door continued to open.

Mrs Crowley called out, 'It's probably just a floorboard, Major. This dismal place is falling to pieces. Small wonder they left it to rot.'

Sheba crouched behind the door of the dark room she had dashed into. Pyewacket jumped into her arms and she held him in a tight squeeze. Beside her, Sister Moon had dropped to a fighting crouch and was drawing her knives from their scabbards, slowly and silently.

Out in the corridor, she heard the man Mrs Crowley had called the Major taking careful steps forward. She imagined his single eye sliding from shadow to shadow like a hawk's, that bloodied weapon ready to slice whatever he found.

She could smell the sword's scent growing stronger and stronger as he approached. *We should have closed the door behind us*, she thought. *We might as well have put a sign outside saying 'We're in here!'* As the fear and adrenalin built up inside her, Sheba felt the fur thickening on her face. Claws started to poke from her fingertips, digging into Pyewacket's back where she held him. He gave a little yelp of pain.

Immediately the footsteps halted. The Major's breathing paused as he listened. After the longest ten seconds in the history of time, he began to move again. This time there was no doubt he was coming towards their door.

Sister Moon had her knives out now. She gave Sheba a grim look, those blank, black eyes glistening in the light from the hallway. Sheba's mind raced. Would Moon be able to take the Major on her own? What could she and Pyewacket do to help?

She was finding it hard to think, as her wolfish instincts began to take over. An urge to rush out and launch herself at the Major – to protect her friends at all costs. But the human part of her knew she would last less than a heartbeat. *Maybe we could escape out of the window*, she thought. *Or Pyewacket could climb down and raise the alarm* . . .

But before she could even move, there was a squeaking sound at her feet. At first, she thought it was a creaky floorboard. Until something black and furry ran across her toes. It dashed past Sister Moon and out through the open doorway, causing the Major to shout in surprise.

One of Mama Rat's little darlings!

Sheba felt a brief surge of relief. Then she heard the sound of sharp metal swishing down.

Thunk.

There was a shrill squeak, then silence.

'What is it?' came Mrs Crowley's muffled voice from the next room.

'Just a rat,' said the Major. His voice was so loud, he must have been inches from the door behind which they were hiding. 'A very big one.'

'A rat? Curse this dismal hole of a house!'

More footsteps as the Major returned to the study. He must have taken the rat's body with him, as there was a squeal of disgust, followed by a coo of delight.

'What a specimen!' said Mrs Crowley's brother. 'May I have it? For medical purposes, of course.'

'You are welcome to it, Professor,' said the Major.

'Just get it out of my sight!' said Mrs Crowley. 'I think we should be departing, anyway. I'm sure you both have final preparations to put in place, and I have some guards to bribe. Did you cash in our last diamond, Major?'

'I did.'

'Then everything rests on a successful hunt tomorrow night. Come.'

Footsteps could be heard leaving the room and walking down the main staircase. There were more voices, as the other wounded men joined them, and then silence.

The children didn't move a muscle until they heard the front door shut. They stayed frozen for a good few minutes to make sure the house was empty. Only then did Sister Moon put her knives away, and Pyewacket peeled himself out of Sheba's arms.

'That poor rat,' whispered Sheba. She felt her eyes begin to prickle with tears. 'Which one was it?'

'I can never tell,' said Pyewacket. 'They're covered in too much soot and grease.'

'Such brave creatures,' whispered Sister Moon. 'They must have followed us from the penny gaff. They were taking care of us all along. I think that one might have been Matthew. He was the ringmaster.'

'What are we going to say to her?' Sheba knew how upset Mama Rat would be. The rats were like her babies. And it had been *her* stupid idea to come here. It was her fault one of the rats had been killed. In fact, she had nearly got them all killed.

Sister Moon squeezed Sheba's shoulder. 'Don't worry about it now. We've got to get back for the show, or there'll be even more trouble.'

In a daze, they tiptoed out of the room and down the stairs. Somehow, they made it out through the back door in silence, then began the frantic dash back to Brick Lane.

CHAPTER THIRTEEN

In which Plumpscuttle becomes a victim.

That evening's show was the most dismal ever. Gigantus, still under the effects of Spindlecrank's poisoned dart, couldn't lift a finger, let alone anything else. Pyewacket hid himself in a corner of his cage, and Sheba spent the entire time trying not to cry. Mama Rat managed to get her rats to put on some kind of a performance, but there was no ratty ringmaster, and every time she thought about it she burst into sobs. Sister Moon even stumbled, when she was zipping through the darkness, and knocked one of her audience clean off his feet.

Sheba felt too guilty to even try apologising. After the show was done, after Plumpscuttle had gone, she would find a way of expressing her sorrow to Mama Rat. But before then she had to sit through two long hours of being stared at.

To make matters even worse, Plumpscuttle's nephew made the unfortunate mistake of letting an old lady in for half price.

'I don't care if someone has actually been *chopped in half* – you still charge them the same as everyone else! Do you understand, you snivelling little snot-stain?' Plumpscuttle steamed about the front room, spittle flying, venting his rage on them all. His face went a shade of purple Sheba had never seen before.

'I'm sorry, Uncle. Can I go home now?'

'Home? *Home?* I'll jolly well send you home!' Plumpscuttle grabbed his nephew by the ear and hoisted him to the front door, which he yanked open with his other hand. Then he booted the boy in the buttocks, sending him flying into the street. There was a fading squeal, followed by a thud. Plumpscuttle slammed the door.

'And as for *you* lot, what in the name of Queen Vic's nightie do you call that? Performing rats that can barely do handstands? A strongman who can't even lift an eyebrow? A lightning-quick shadow that's slower than a snail? A grotesque hidden under a pile of straw and a wolfgirl who cries instead of snarls? I'll tell you what: after I've finished my evening's activities, I'm going to start making enquiries about a new lot of acts. Ones that do what's flipping well asked of them!'

He gave them all a final glare, then stormed out of the house, banging the door so hard that the windows shook in their frames.

There was silence in the front room for a good few minutes after that. Finally, they moved to huddle round the fireplace. Sheba went to Mama Rat, tears spilling out of her eyes and soaking into the fur on her cheeks. Getting Matthew killed was the worst thing she'd ever done. *If Mama Rat never speaks to me again, I deserve it*, she thought.

But Mama just took her by the shoulders and pulled her into a tight hug. Sheba was overcome. It was the first ever hug she could remember. Being so close to someone was overpowering to begin with, but warm and safe as well. She snuggled further into Mama Rat's arms, breathing deep the smell of pipe smoke, lavender and rodent.

'I'm so sorry,' she sobbed into Mama Rat's shoulder.

'It's not your fault, dearie. I know you didn't mean him to come to harm.'

'But you lot shouldn't have gone off on your own like that,' said Gigantus. 'These are dangerous people we're dealing with.'

'They weren't to know that, were they?' Mama Rat said.

'Even so . . .'

'It's my fault,' said Sister Moon. She bowed her head in shame. 'I told them I knew what to do.'

'But it was my idea,' said Sheba. 'If anyone's to blame, it's me.'

'I'd just like to point out that I was against it all along,' said Pyewacket.

'It doesn't matter whose idea it was,' said Mama Rat. 'The only people to blame are that Crowley woman and her henchmen. How that cold-hearted cow could use the idea of a dead child to trick us . . .

Anyway, that's beside the point. The next time you get it into your heads to do something like that, we all go together. Understood?'

The three young carnival acts all nodded their heads sheepishly, before each went to help take down the sheets and lanterns from the show. By the time they had finished, Sheba felt too tired to think about what they'd learned from Mrs Crowley's house, too tired even to worry about Till. She left the others sitting around the fireplace and trudged up to the bedroom.

She sat on the edge of her mattress, not knowing what to do with herself. Crawling into bed was tempting, but she knew it would be a long time before she fell asleep. Time which her mind would spend replaying horrid scenes from the evening: the Major creeping towards her hiding place, the awful sound of his blade slicing through poor Matthew . . .

She needed a distraction. Then she noticed that Gigantus had already rolled out his bedding. Beneath it, the telltale lump of his book could be seen. Perhaps a spot of Agnes Throbbington might cheer her up. Before she could convince herself it was a bad idea, she had slid the heavy book out and was opening it to a new page.

. . . Agnes strolled along the high street on a beautiful summer's morning. Her head was dizzy with thoughts, mostly about how beautiful she was. 'I really do deserve to be married to someone incredibly handsome and wealthy,' she said to herself. She was growing bored of Jeremy Gristle.

She scanned the crowds that filled the street. She was looking out for someone spectacular enough to match her. And then she saw him.

Stepping out of a coffee shop, he positively gleamed in his bright red captain's uniform.

Agnes's heart did a backflip. She knew without a trace of doubt that this man was her one true love. She almost swooned when she saw him walking towards her, but she conveniently managed to control herself until he was near enough to catch her in his manly, manly arms.

'My lady,' he said, 'you seem to be suffering from the summer sun. Permit me to assist you.'

'Why, thank you,' Agnes gasped. 'Gosh, you're awfully strong, aren't you?'

'Allow me to introduce myself. I am Captain Cedric Spingly-Spongton of the 3rd Light Dragoons.'

'Captain, you say,' sighed Agnes. 'You must be the son of a very rich and noble lord or something?'

'Alas, I am afraid not, ma'am. My family are but poor farmers from Dorset. But now I have drunk of your beauty, I count myself among the richest men in the—'

'Yes, yes, all right,' said Agnes, pushing him away and checking he hadn't ruffled her perfect hair. 'If you don't mind, I have dresses to buy; I don't have time to stand about talking to paupers. Kindly shove off, you countrified oaf.'

And she flounced off down the street.

Sheba managed a half smile as she tucked the book back under Gigantus's mattress. The writings of Gertrude Lacygusset had helped a little. For a moment, she even considered letting Gigantus know she had enjoyed it. But then she realised he would probably be furious at her for prying. She had caused more than enough upset already that evening. With a sigh, she began to get ready for bed.

It was only when she took off her cape that she realised it was missing. She searched every pocket in turn, finding hairpins, Spindlecrank's pistol, Till's chipped marble – but no sign whatsoever of Mrs Crowley's calling card.

A sick wave of fear slowly spread outwards from her stomach.

She could have dropped it anywhere along the way back from Paradise Street. She could have. But a part of her was ice-cold certain that she hadn't. She had dropped the card in Mrs Crowley's house, behind the door where they had hidden.

She might not find it, Sheba told herself. *She might never go in that room, never think to look behind the door.*

But it was no use trying to convince herself. She had just announced to a murderous villain that she had been spying in her house as clearly as if she had strolled up and left a calling card of her own.

*

They all gathered around the breakfast table the

next morning and sipped their coffee in silence. Somewhere in the yard Pyewacket could be heard waking up. An unpleasant mixture of coughing, spitting and scratching, followed by the clang of his cage door as he clambered out. Flossy and Raggety were making noises too: whickering and bleating that meant their breakfast oats were long overdue. Sheba normally fed them first thing, but today she hadn't the energy.

After the tragedy of losing Matthew, nobody had mentioned what they had discovered at Mrs Crowley's house. The information had cost a great deal, and it was important. Vitally important. Sheba was wondering about the most tactful way to bring it up when Pyewacket hopped onto the kitchen windowsill, making everyone except Sister Moon jump and spill their coffee.

'I have consulted the ether,' he announced, 'and decided today is the day we tell the police all about that Mrs Crowley. And we can add "rat-murdering" to her list of crimes.'

Mama Rat mopped at the fresh tears in her eyes.

'Did you have to bring that up again, you

thoughtless pixie?' Gigantus glared at him.

'We don't have any evidence to prove she's done anything wrong,' said Sister Moon. 'And killing rats isn't a crime, I'm afraid.'

Mama Rat sniffed again. 'It should be. Didn't you lot discover anything worthwhile last night?'

'Well . . . we overheard some plans,' said Sheba. She put her coffee down and began to give her account.

Mama Rat and Gigantus nodded as she told them about the old house by the river and the sinister meeting which took place there. As she neared the end, it occurred to her that she could leave out the part about the dropped calling card. Nobody need ever know except her. But that would be a kind of lie: a dishonesty to her friends. She decided they deserved to know, so she confessed that also, even though it was almost in a whisper.

'Don't worry,' said Sister Moon. 'The card could have fallen out anywhere. And even if she did find it, Mrs Crowley wouldn't know it was yours. She must give out lots of cards.'

'But if she *does* turn up here to get us, it's completely your fault,' said Pyewacket.

'So, to sum up,' said Gigantus, ignoring Pyewacket, 'Mrs Crowley isn't a grieving mother at all. And she's working with these two sinister men for some reason we don't yet know.'

'If it involves a rat-killing monster and some kind of professor, it can't be anything good,' said Mama Rat.

Sheba nodded. 'Crowley's brother, the professor – if he even is one – didn't smell like an educated man. He stank of death and rot and evil things.'

'Maybe he studies chopped-up bodies,' said Sister Moon. 'Like the doctors Large 'Arry told us about.'

'Monkey bodies, certainly,' said Pyewacket. 'Don't forget, he was the one that gave them to Spindlecrank so she could build those clockwork . . . things.'

'Well, whoever they are,' continued Gigantus, 'they need several children and something important – whatever that is. They got Spindlecrank to build them a machine (which must have cost them a pretty penny) and snatched a bunch of mudlarks that they thought no one would miss. Now all they need to do is get one more child and this item they want, and they can do . . .' He paused, looking stumped. 'Well, whatever it is they have planned.'

'Well done, Inspector Flea-Brain,' said Pyewacket.

'There are so many questions still to answer,' added Sister Moon.

'But I don't understand,' said Sheba. 'What could they need the children for? And where do the deserting soldiers come into it?'

'Let's take one thing at a time,' said Mama Rat. 'We should focus on what we actually know for now. Didn't you say it was tonight's low tide they were going to snatch another mudlark?'

'Yes,' Sheba nodded. 'We need to stop them. And find out where she is keeping the others.'

'They're not in the house,' said Mama Rat. 'While Matthew was . . . was helping you, the others gave the place a quick going over. No sign of any children. Not even in the cellar.'

'But there must be a reason she's living in that tatty house,' said Sheba. 'The place and her just don't fit. I'm sure it's something to do with the river.'

Sister Moon had been standing still for a long while, frowning in thought. She slowly raised a finger. 'I have an idea,' she said. 'A way to stop the machine and find the children. But I need certain objects—'

Before she could say any more, the front door burst open with a crash.

They all leaped out of their seats and rushed into the parlour in time to see the battered form of Plumpscuttle stagger in from the street. He was never the picture of health when he returned from a night on the town, but now he looked like one of the walking dead. In fact, a corpse that had been murdered, buried and then brought back to life would have looked quite a bit healthier.

His face was swollen and bruised. Dried blood spattered his torn shirt. One eye was puffed up into a tiny slit. And he appeared to have lost some teeth.

'Set upon!' he cried, collapsing into the battered armchair by the fireplace. 'Set upon by hoodlums and footpads! Someone tried to kill me!'

'Slow down, dearie, and tell us who did this to you.' Mama Rat tried to examine his wounds as he writhed and groaned. He'd clearly been given a serious beating.

'Some thugs,' he yelled. 'Some brutes with eye

patches and bandages! They caught me on the way to Mrs Crobbin's gin parlour and pounded me into pieces! Then they told me to give this to my friends . . . stupid idiots! I don't have any friends!'

Plumpscuttle held something up in his blood-spattered hands, and then passed out with a final groan. As he lay senseless, dribbling into his neckerchief, Sister Moon reached down to pry open his fingers and remove the tattered thing he had been clutching.

It was a piece of card, now dotted with spots of Plumpscuttle's blood. Even as Moon handed it to her, Sheba knew what it would be.

It was Mrs Crowley's calling card, still creased with the fold she had made with her own fingers.

CHAPTER FOURTEEN

In which our friends set a fiendish trap.

Low tide came just after midnight and, had anyone been walking beside the banks of the Thames, they would have been treated to a rare sight. A group of odd-shaped figures, all in black, were apparently about to drown a long-armed urchin dressed in filthy rags, with a length of rope dangling from his waist.

'You can't do this!' the urchin shouted. 'It's a full moon! That's a bad omen for children and people with long arms!'

'You're just making that up. As usual.' Gigantus held Pyewacket in an iron grip. The big man was grinning. 'How far out do you want me to toss him?' he said to the others. 'I reckon I could send him a good thirty feet.'

'If you don't put me down right now, I'm going to summon a horde of hobgoblins!' yelled Pyewacket. 'I'll make them eat your toes off!'

They stood at the high-tide line on the south bank, next to an upturned skiff. They had chosen a spot just upriver from Paradise Street, guessing that the crab machine would strike as close to home as possible. Sheba still had no idea where the thing was kept but, as all the attacks had been in this area, she reckoned it must be near the villains' home.

She looked around at her friends. The pale faces of Gigantus and Mama Rat bobbed about in the darkness like disembodied turnips. Sister Moon was holding a rusty whaling harpoon that they had discovered in an old ironmonger's on Spicers Street. Attached to it was a whisky bottle filled with white phosphorus: a gloopy liquid which gave out a dim glow, like trapped starlight.[xxv]

A wide stretch of mud lay before them, glistening silver beneath the moon. The water beyond sparkled.

It was almost beautiful, until you looked close enough to see what was floating in it.

'Don't worry,' Sheba said to Pyewacket. 'There's really no danger. At the first sign of anything bad, Gigantus will haul on the rope and drag you back here to safety. You just have to stand on the mud for a few minutes. You'll be helping. Till and all the mudlarks could be saved because of you.'

'But I don't want to save anyone! I should be home, in my cage, staring into my crystal b— Aaaaaaaaaaargh!'

Before Pyewacket could finish his sentence, Gigantus launched him like a human javelin. He flew through the night air, trailing a terrified squeal, and landed with a wet smack right beside the water's edge.

'You didn't have to throw him quite so hard, Gigantus,' said Mama Rat.

The ungainly figure struggled to right itself in the smelly slop, then began wailing and trying to wade back to shore.

'Stay there, you putrid little munchkin!' called Gigantus, 'or I won't bother to pull you back in when whatever-it-is comes for you!'

'You're really enjoying this, aren't you?' came Sister Moon's voice from somewhere in the darkness.

'Oh, yes,' said Gigantus happily. 'It was an excellent plan of yours.'

'Well, the trap is set,' said Mama Rat. 'We must take our positions.'

There was a slight rattling of pebbles as Moon stole away. An instant later, Sheba thought she saw her slip underneath a jetty which stretched out into the river. Just a ripple among the shadows.

'Good luck, everyone,' Sheba whispered, and saw Gigantus nod as he and Mama Rat ducked behind the old skiff.

When Sister Moon had outlined her plan in the house that afternoon, it had sounded like a stroke of genius. Out here in the cold night, in the mud, where clawed, child-snatching machines lurked, it seemed half-baked and flimsy.

Sheba took a deep breath and set off on her own mission.

*

At first, everyone had been reluctant to let her go alone. The streets of London weren't a good place for anybody to be unaccompanied, especially a child. However, as she had pointed out, most children didn't carry a pistol full of poisoned darts. *And most children can't turn into snarling, snapping wolfgirls, either.*

As she climbed the steps up from the river and started making her way downstream along the Bermondsey Wall, she began to wish she hadn't been so keen. When Sister Moon suggested they would need someone to watch the river between the jetty and Paradise Street, to see if the creature returned there, Sheba volunteered. She did have the best senses of hearing and smell. And besides, the only other alternative was being the decoy. She was quite happy to leave that job to Pyewacket.

But now it came to walking through the dark towards Paradise Street all alone, she didn't feel anywhere near as brave. She wished she was still clutching at Gigantus's woolly jersey. Her stomach flipped at every tiny sound. Underneath the river stink, scents flooded her nose. Soot and coal dust, gas and the ever-present reek of raw sewage. Her heart pounded in her chest. She could feel her fur bristling and her nose stretching, her teeth growing and her eyes burning orange. Just like when she was angry, fear seemed to bring out the wolf in her.

Sheba slipped through the shadows. She didn't want to stumble into anyone while she looked like this. People might find it amazing when they were paying to see it, but bumping into a snarling half-wolf down a dark alley was another matter.

Eventually, she came to a set of narrow stone stairs that led down to the river. Directly behind her was Paradise Street. If they were right, Mrs Crowley had needed a place close to the river for a reason: so that Spindlecrank's machine could get in and out of the mud without being seen.

Half of her wanted to find the crab machine's hideout, half prayed she would never have to set eyes on it. Wondering which part would get its wish, Sheba gritted her sharp white teeth and set off down the steps.

*

Somewhere across the river, a church clock chimed one. The stakeout on the mudflats had now been running for the best part of an hour.

Out on the mud, the bait had grown tired of flailing and was now slowly sinking up to its knees, whining in a pitiful manner. Gigantus, from his position behind the skiff, had long ceased being amused and was now just cold and tired. Mama Rat was beginning to worry their plan had failed, which meant another victim might have been taken elsewhere along the river.

Crouching beneath the jetty, Sister Moon was the only one still focused. She had tucked her dark glasses away in her waistcoat pocket and was staring out at the water with her jet-black eyes. They drank in every last scrap of light, marked each tiny ripple and current that ebbed around the sorry figure of Pyewacket. The harpoon in her hands was poised, ready for flight.

And lucky for Pyewacket it was, too. Because something was beginning to stir in the silt beneath him. Almost imperceptible at first; a slight vibration in the jelly-like mud around his legs. Then bubbles began to pop on the surface, followed by a red rubber exhaust pipe that puffed a trail of steam . . .

Sister Moon raised the harpoon higher.

With a sudden roar, the mud beneath Pyewacket collapsed. A spiked dome heaved itself to the surface. Claws clacked and snapped as they freed themselves from the sticky slime, tearing at Pyewacket's ragged trousers, and all was lit by the glow from a yellow porthole in the centre. A porthole in which the Major's face could be seen, his teeth bared in a fierce grin.

Pyewacket screamed.

And Moon flung the harpoon, aiming for the thinnest of lines on the creature's back: an overlap of its armour plating. A line that nobody else would have been able to see in the dark, let alone in the space of a heartbeat. The rusty tip slid into the crab like a dart into butter, jamming itself firmly in place.

Gigantus, startled into action, heaved on the rope – with a little too much zeal. Pyewacket shot out of the creature's grasp, flew high over the open mudflat and crunched straight into the side of the skiff with a smack.

A wail of grinding gears came from the creature. It sank slowly into the mud, pulling the harpoon with it. The end jutted out for a moment, the bottle of phosphorus swinging to and fro, before disappearing with the rest. As the ripples of soupy water slowly stilled, drops of the white substance could be seen glowing in the moonlight.

The crab had been tagged.

*

Sheba sat at the foot of the narrow stone steps, her feet resting on the slime of the riverbank. She could hear the water lapping at the mud as the tide crawled slowly in. The night was drawing to a close, and the river was readying itself for another busy day.

Somewhere, a steamer chuffed along. Wisps of fog had started drifting past, making ghostly shapes in the moonlight. Swirls and loops that became smudged faces with waving arms. It made Sheba shiver, prickled the fur on her neck. She tried to ignore it by unpicking the mystery that was Mrs Crowley.

It was impossible to know what that woman was up to. She must have lured them to the graveyard just to get a look at who was nosing into her business. All that rubbish about her son had been nothing but a pack of lies (the fact Sheba had fallen for it so easily still smarted), but why was she taking so many children? And why only the tatty, half-starved waifs of the riverside? In fact, why had Mrs Crowley given *Sheba* the card?

Was the frizzy-haired professor really her brother? And why were the Major and his friends working with her? Sheba remembered what she had heard in the Paradise Street study: *We shall have what we most desire. And how long we have waited . . .* What was it they wanted so badly?

The questions wouldn't stop. She thought so hard that her furry little head throbbed. Still, they only had to prove Mrs Crowley had taken the children, and then they could call in the police and let them deal with it. She was just picturing Mrs Crowley being led away in iron handcuffs when her attention was caught by a movement downriver.

She peered into the darkness. Something was

pushing up out of the mud. It was difficult to make out, but it appeared to be enormous, spiky and slicked with slime. *The crab machine!* Some kind of rod was jutting out of its back, and it was making a high-pitched, keening sound. A forlorn whine of grinding metal. Before she could get a better look, a wave of thicker fog blew across her line of sight.

Sheba cursed. She was supposed to be following it and now she couldn't even *see* it. She would have to march through the mist and hope she didn't walk right into it. Taking a deep breath for courage, she began to edge downriver, along the bank.

The fog had really set in now, and every step she took sent her deeper into the blankness. She could barely see her own toes. She held her breath, ready to run screaming at the slightest movement. It was difficult to judge exactly where she was going, but by counting her steps she estimated she had walked ten yards or so when she came across a gaping crater in the mud. It was releasing waves of stink so strong that Sheba nearly keeled over backwards. She clamped her handkerchief over her nose and peered at what she could see of the ground.

There were droplets of glowing white liquid on the crater's surface, leading up the bank to a crumbling brick wall and into a rank-smelling tunnel. The entrance was partly hidden by rotten planks of wood, slimy weeds and a rusty grate. It looked (and smelled) just like any other sewer outlet along the riverbank. Sheba would never have spotted it, had it not been for the phosphorus. *That Sister Moon knows a few tricks*, she thought.

Note where the trail leads, and nothing more. That's what Mama Rat had said. But it couldn't hurt if she had a tiny peek. Could it?

Holding her breath, Sheba slipped behind the stack of rotting timber and pulled open the rusty grate. It squealed noisily and she winced, but there was now enough space for her to squeeze through. The white drops continued up the tunnel; she could see them glowing well into the distance. She took a careful step into the tunnel mouth, then stopped. The grate swung shut behind her. She couldn't be sure, but it looked like part of the glowing trail had *moved*.

Sheba froze. Her heart skipped a beat. There was a scraping sound from further up the shaft, and the

drops shifted again. Slowly it came to her: the very
furthest spots of light weren't part of the trail . . .
phosphorus had splashed over the thing's back . . .
The crab was still in the tunnel!

She turned and ran to the grate. But it was now
jammed in place. From behind her, she could hear
the sound of metal scraping against the stonework,
getting louder and closer by the second. The fur on
her neck was standing up. She began to growl. There
was the chuff of an engine and the clank of broken
machinery.

Her claws were out. She grabbed the grate and
pushed with all her strength. She could smell it now:
hot oil and smoke, river mud and coal dust. For a
terrible moment she thought the grate wasn't going
to shift, then suddenly it gave way and she tumbled
free of the tunnel mouth, landing on her face in the
slimy weeds outside. *I'm safe*, she thought. *All I have
to do is get back to the others and tell them where
the tunnel is.*

She heaved herself up on all fours, ready to run,
when she felt something close around her ankle.

Something cold, hard, serrated . . .

The crab had reached out a claw and grabbed her. With irresistible, mechanical strength, it began to pull her in.

Sheba let out one terrified, growling shriek before she was hauled out of sight, back into the dark.

CHAPTER FIFTEEN

In which Sheba finds herself caged
once more.

Sheba was woken by a dim light. At first she thought she was in her bed at Brick Lane, and that the night before had been some awful nightmare. Her body soon told her otherwise.

She was frozen to the bone, both dress and cloak clinging in damp, icy folds. Her ankle felt as though it had been run through a mangle;[xxvi] crushed and bruised, stinging where the claw had broken the skin. There was a lump on the side of her head that throbbed each time she moved. Everything was stiff and sore.

Beneath her she could feel slimy stone. If it was

daylight that had roused her, then she must have been knocked out cold for the whole night.

With a burst of effort that made flashes appear before her eyes, Sheba pushed herself upright and looked around. She was in some kind of chamber. The faint rays of daylight came from the left. *Must be the tunnel entrance*, she thought. All she could smell was the filthy stink of the river and the rusty scent of hot metal and steam.

She tried to raise a hand to the bump on her head, and then panicked. She couldn't. Then she realised her hands had been tied together at the wrist. Coarse rope burnt her furry skin, and her fingertips tingled where the circulation had been cut off. She stretched out her bound hands and touched a series of vertical iron bars.

She was in a cage. Again.

Many people would have found this a terrifying discovery, but Sheba had spent most of her life locked away. There was a stone wall behind her; she leant back on it and calmly assessed her situation.

The crab had caught her last night, and its pilot – the Major, she assumed – had tied her up and thrown her in a cage. She had found the crab's secret hideaway, but the knowledge was useless unless she could tell someone.

Sheba patted her pockets. Whoever had bound her had not thought to search her first. She still had her hairpins and the clockwork pistol. Hopefully it would work despite the damp. Could she manage to pick the lock with her hands tied? Maybe she could use her claws to scratch through her rope bindings.

A sudden noise beside her made her jump. Peering into the gloom, she could make out vague shapes. There seemed to be more cages. Six or seven at least. In the one next to her, a small, dark bundle was stirring.

'Hello?' she whispered. 'Is anyone there?'

The bundle of rags twitched some more, and then Sheba saw the glint of two large, blinking eyes.

'Hello?' Sheba tried again. Then she frowned. Was there a familiar scent under the rank stench of river mud? 'Is . . . is that you, Till?'

'Who are you?' The voice that came from the ragged lump was cracked and broken. Its owner hadn't spoken for a long while, but the words were enough for Sheba to recognise her friend.

'It's me. Sheba. The girl from the sideshow. The one with . . . with the hair.'

The lump moved some more, growing one spindly white arm, then another, and gradually unfolding into the shape of a tiny girl. She shuffled forward, her bony fingers clutching the iron bars of her cage.

'Sheba?' The hope in her voice was almost painful to hear. 'But . . . what are you doing here? Did the monster get you?'

Sheba slid over to the bars, ignoring the sudden pain in her head and ankle. She lifted her bound hands and put them over Till's.

'Till! I'm so glad I've found you! We've been searching and searching for days.'

'You've been searching for me?' Till blinked in surprise. 'But I only met you once. Why would you come looking for me?'

'Because . . . because you were nice to me.' Sheba didn't know how to explain that nobody *normal* had ever shown kindness to her before. It made her feel embarrassed somehow. Cemented the fact she felt so different. She tried to change the subject. 'And your parents, they came to us and asked us to help.'

'My parents?' Till's eyes glistened and sparkled in the gloom.

Sheba gave the girl's fingers a gentle squeeze. 'Yes, they've been looking too. But it's all right now. I've found you. I can tell them where you are.'

'And 'ow are you going to do that, when you're locked in 'ere?' said another voice from somewhere else inside the chamber.

Sheba jumped, fearing it might be Mrs Crowley – even though she hadn't smelled her – but whoever it was sounded as tired, weak and terrified as Till.

'There's more of us here,' Till explained. 'Eight others. We all got taken by the monster. We've tried to escape, but there's no way out.'

'There is now,' Sheba said. 'I just have to get these ropes off.'

'It's no good,' said Till. 'The cages are locked. And they come to check on us all the time. If they think we've been trying to escape, they beat us.'

'Who are they?' Sheba asked.

'We call her the Night Lady,' said Till, 'the one

what wears black. Her and the tall man with the patch. And sometimes there's another. A man with white hair and spectacles. He doesn't hit us, though. He just prods us and measures us with his devices.'

Sheba absorbed this information. 'Have they said anything to you? Told you why you were taken?'

Till shook her head. 'They don't speak to us much. The Night Lady just laughs when we cry. Then she gets the patched man to hit us. It's better if you don't make a sound.'

'I've heard them, though,' another voice called out. This one came from the black murk at the far end of the chamber. 'I been here the longest, see. Back when there was just me, I heard them talking together. About something they wanted. A prize, they said. In Hyde Park.'

Sheba recalled the conversation from Paradise Street. *Are you sure you will be able to get it?* the professor had said. *They have it very well guarded . . .* Whatever they were after was in Hyde Park. She was about to ask what was so special about the place when she remembered Mama Rat's newspaper. The Great Exhibition was in Hyde Park.[xxvii]

Were they going to rob the Crystal Palace? What for? She racked her aching head for what she could remember of the exhibits. The crystal fountain? No, too big. One of the sculptures? Or a machine? None seemed worth all this trouble. Something Mrs Crowley most desired, she had said. What did grown-ups most desire? Money? Fame? Gold? Jewels . . . ?

'Was it a jewel?' she asked. 'Did the Night Lady mention a diamond?'

There was a moment's silence from the cages, then one of the children spoke.

'She might have,' they said.

'I think she did,' called another.

The Koh-i-noor. That had to be it. Mrs Crowley was going after the world's largest diamond. Maybe they were going to make the children steal it.

'We have to get out of here,' Sheba whispered to Till.

'But I told you,' Till whispered back. 'There's no way out. The cages are locked.'

'Not for long,' said Sheba. She began to wriggle and turn her wrists, ignoring the stinging and chafing, trying to loosen the rope so she could get her hands free. In her panic, she could feel the wolf inside her growing. But instead of holding back, she let it snarl; welcoming the extra dose of strength and ferocity it gave her.

The rope ripped hair from her arms and burnt her skin, but she kept pulling and pulling. Eventually she felt it begin to loosen a fraction. A bit more and she'd be able to slip a hand free.

A booming clang echoed from somewhere beyond the chamber. It was followed by voices, distant at first, but growing rapidly closer.

'They're coming!' Till hissed, dashing to the back of her cage. 'Sheba, they're coming!'

There was the shrill sound of squeaking hinges, and the grating of ancient wood on stone. Somewhere a door was being opened. Sheba strained to see, and was instantly blinded by a flare of searing light. Falling backwards, hands pressed over her face, she thought there had been some kind of silent explosion, but as she peered through her fingers she could see it was only the light from a lantern.

There were three figures. Without much surprise, she recognised Mrs Crowley, the Major with his half-covered face and the frizzy-haired professor, her brother. She could smell the professor's twisted medical stink, and the bloodied metal sword of the other. His coat was open, and his hand rested on the hilt as he glared around the chamber. Perhaps he was angry that they had speared his machine.

She also noticed the dark passageway they had stepped from. Where did it lead? Back to Paradise Street? *I knew there was a reason for her staying there. She can walk from the house to this place without being seen.* The fact she had been right didn't give Sheba much satisfaction now.

Mrs Crowley paused to light a torch on the wall. Now Sheba could see they were indeed in a large chamber made of heavy stone. Ribbed arches supported the roof. They looked ancient, crumbling. A row of cages stretched around the wall, each one holding the small, shivering body of a child. To her left was the tunnel entrance, a soft glow in the dark. Down there, just a short dash away, were the river, her friends, her freedom. But it might as well have been a trek of a hundred miles.

Right in front of the cages was a wide pit. Steps led down to a muddy lagoon, where the mechanical crab floated. Hooked chains on pulleys stretched up to the ceiling, holding it in place. Sheba could clearly see Sister Moon's whaling harpoon jutting out of the crab's back. She had thrown it perfectly: its barbed tip had sunk straight into the machinery inside. Even now, smoke was slowly seeping from beneath its carapace, while thick oil dribbled into the water, spreading out in a rainbow-slicked pool. It looked dead, if that could be true of something that had never really lived. It was broken, at any rate. If Sheba hadn't achieved anything else, at least it wouldn't be snatching any more mudlarks from the river.

'A harpoon? I don't believe it,' Mrs Crowley said. Her lisping voice echoed around the stone room, making Sheba jump. 'Has the thing been badly damaged?'

'I can't get it to work any more,' said the Major. 'Not without Spindlecrank—'

'Those interfering buffoons!' Mrs Crowley slammed her lantern down on the floor, cracking the glass. It was the first time Sheba had seen a dent in her cool exterior. 'I thought you said you'd warned them off? Didn't you beat their leader hard enough?'

The Major shrugged. Sheba wondered who they meant by 'leader'. Then she realised it was Plumpscuttle. If she hadn't been scared out of her wits, she might have laughed.

'Where is the one you captured?'

The Major pointed to Sheba's cage.

Mrs Crowley walked towards her – it was as if a shadow had peeled itself from the wall. Under the featureless veil, Sheba imagined a face twisted in rage. But instead of cowering back, she rose to her knees, snarling and showing her fangs. She could smell the woman's familiar odour again. That scent she couldn't quite place. A flower? A plant? A perfume? It was definitely something she had smelled before. But where?

The veiled woman paused outside the cage and seemed to be staring at her again, just like she had in the graveyard. It was a different kind of stare to the ones Sheba usually got. More intense. She could almost feel the woman thinking as the seconds of silence ticked by.

She's probably deciding on the best place to kick me, Sheba thought. But when Mrs Crowley spoke, her voice was calm. She sounded almost amused.

'It's the little girl, is it? The rat woman's pet. Were you the one snooping around my house, or was it one of your . . . *malformed* friends?' The woman almost spat the word, making Sheba wince.

'It was me,' said Sheba. Let her take whatever punishment this horrid woman would give, if it meant the others would be left alone.

'On your own? I hardly think so. I suppose you expect me to believe you threw the harpoon that ruined my machine as well?'

'No, but I followed the trail.'

Mrs Crowley looked again at the crab. The bottle hanging from the harpoon end still trickled drops of phosphorus onto the rusty carapace.

'Very ingenious,' said Mrs Crowley. 'But for all your cunning, it only got you as far as this cage. I would call that a failure, wouldn't you?'

'I know what you're planning,' Sheba said. 'That's not a failure.' It probably wasn't the best thing to blurt out, but the woman was making Sheba angry. She could feel her snout jutting and her ears tweaking into points as her inner wolf began to take over.

Mrs Crowley gave a tinkling laugh. 'Come on, then. Let's hear it.'

'You're going to steal the Koh-i-noor from the Great Exhibition!' Sheba shouted. 'You're going to make the children take it, so they get the blame!'

She half expected Mrs Crowley to scream in frustration. Instead, the woman turned her shrouded face to where the two men stood. The three looked at each other for a few seconds, and then the professor and Mrs Crowley burst out laughing. Even the Major allowed himself a smirk.

Sheba was left speechless. What was so funny? Had she got it wrong?

'I suppose there's a hint of truth there,' Mrs Crowley said, when she had stopped chuckling. 'It would be nice to see the look on your face, when you realise how close you came. Pity that won't be possible, what with you being *dead*. Unless you think we can use her, Euan?'

The bald man shuffled over to her cage and peered at her through his spectacles, which were so thick that his eyes seemed to swim behind them, like two brown goldfish in their bowls. One of his bony hands shot through the bars and grabbed the crown of her head. Sheba could feel his fingers squeezing and prodding at her skull.

'No, I'm afraid the material would be too tainted,' he said, at last. 'It might hinder the properties of the formula.'

Formula? What was the man talking about? And what did her head have to do with it? Try as she might, Sheba couldn't understand what they meant.

'Shame,' said Mrs Crowley. Her lisp made the word sound like a snake hissing. 'We shall have to hope what we've already got will be enough. We have no time to collect any more: everything is in place for tonight. I have even arranged for several of the Exhibition guards to be elsewhere. You had best start moving the children.'

The professor nodded and went to fetch a ring of heavy iron keys from the wall. Sheba heard herself snarling and growling in frustration. She had only just found Till and now she was being hidden somewhere else.

'Major Kapoor,' Mrs Crowley called. 'These carnival freaks have become a serious nuisance.

Fetch your men and pay them a visit. I want them all dead before tonight's proceedings, just in case they try to get in the way.'

'No!' screamed Sheba. The thought of her friends being harmed made her fling herself at the cage bars over and over. 'Leave them alone, you evil witch! Leave them alone!'

'And as for this one . . .' Mrs Crowley paused on her way out of the chamber. She seemed to be considering something. Finally she shook her head and pressed a hand to her brow. 'Stake her out in the tunnel. The tide is coming in. It should make short work of her.'

'With pleasure,' said the Major. He moved towards Sheba's cage, half a smile poking out from behind his patch.

'Oh, and Major?' Mrs Crowley called back from the door. 'Be careful. She bites.'

Chapter Sixteen

*In which the carnival has to battle
for survival.*

Following his instructions, the Major dragged her from the cage and tied her to iron stakes hammered into the tunnel floor. At first, Sheba thought she might be able to pull them out after he had gone. The ground was only river mud and pebbles, after all.

She soon found she was wrong. The stakes were long – they bit deep enough to reach through the soft mud and into something harder and less yielding. She tried heaving at each of the pegs that held her arms and legs in turn, but they wouldn't budge. Not even when she got scared and felt her wolfish strength surge.

Next, she tried screaming. The river wasn't far away – the horns of steamships and cries of bargemen echoed up the tunnel. Surely somebody would hear her and come to investigate?

Sheba yelled until her throat was raw.

Nobody came.

So now she lay on her back, looking up at the slimy brickwork above her. Water was steadily filling the passageway. She could feel it seeping under her legs. Maybe only a few inches at the moment, but rising fast. It looked as though she was going to meet her end here, drowned in the stinking Thames water, while a few miles away her friends were chopped into pieces by Major Kapoor and his soldier comrades.

The bodies of the other carnival members might be found – they'd probably get a mention in the newspaper – but she would lie forever in this damp and lonely tunnel. Maybe in two hundred years or so someone would find her bones and wonder why a little girl had been tied down and left for the eels to eat.

She was quietly thinking morbid thoughts to herself, letting her tears trickle down to join the pool of water beneath her, when she felt something move by her foot. Eels already! Sheba shrieked and tried to jerk her leg away, but couldn't. She raised her head, hardly daring to look, expecting to see a slimy face with a mouthful of needle-sharp teeth and blank eyes.

Instead, there was a plump black rat sitting on her shoe, its fur glistening with oily grease and its beady eyes sparkling in the half-light of the tunnel. She hadn't even thought about the rats. The riverside must be thick with them, and they wouldn't bother waiting for her to die before they began feasting. Being eaten alive by rats would really hurt.

'Go away,' Sheba croaked.

The rat gave several loud, piercing squeaks – and more rats scuttled down from the tunnel mouth. Soon there were five of them perched on Sheba's legs. The end had come, then, and there was nothing she could do. But just before she squeezed her eyes shut, waiting for the nibbling to start, she saw the first rat do something extraordinary. It put its paws on its hips and rolled its eyes. Sheba even thought she heard it make a sound like a tut. She felt a tiny flicker of hope.

'Bartholomew?' she said, slowly. 'Judas, Thaddeus, Simon and Peter?'

The rats squeaked and chattered. It was them! Sheba had never thought she'd be so glad to see a pack of vermin.

'Can you get me out of here?' she asked. 'The others are in danger. I have to get back to them!'

The rats instantly dashed to the ropes at her arms and legs and began gnawing. Sheba lay very still as their yellow teeth chewed and chomped. After a few minutes, she felt her left ankle spring free. It wasn't long before the other leg followed, then her hands. She sat up, rubbing at the burnt skin on her wrists, while the rats clustered around, looking up at her with their bright little eyes.

'Thank you so much,' said Sheba. 'That's twice you've saved my life now.' If they hadn't been quite so slime-covered and generally revolting, she could have kissed them. Instead she gave them what she hoped was a grateful smile.

'I have to get to Brick Lane,' she said. 'I don't

suppose you can show me the quickest way?'

The rats instantly scampered off down the tunnel, waiting for Sheba at the entrance. With a groan, she forced herself to stand and began to stagger after them. Her bruised body wanted nothing more than to curl up and sleep, preferably after a warm bath and change of clothes, but she had to warn the others before the Major came for them.

As she limped out of the tunnel that had so nearly become her tomb, she prayed she would be in time.

*

Back at Brick Lane, the others were moping in the yard, when there came a frantic hammering at the gate. Sister Moon opened it a fraction, blade at the ready, and saw a furry, shaggy blob of mud with wild orange eyes and a cluster of rats at its feet. It took her a moment to recognise Sheba.

'You're alive!' Moon shouted, pulling her into the yard and hugging her tightly, despite her coating of stinking muck. 'Sheba, we were so worried!'

The rest of them jumped up and clustered around,

cheering and clapping. The rats dashed up to Mama.

'Well done, my boys! My clever beauties!' she cried.

'There's no time!' Sheba shouted, pushing Sister Moon away. 'Mrs Crowley's servant is coming here right now! He's coming to kill us!'

'But what happened to you?' Gigantus asked, his craggy face creased with worry. 'Where have you been?'

As fast as she was able, Sheba blurted out everything that had happened: following the crab machine's trail, being caught, finding the mudlarks, discovering Mrs Crowley's plan and finally being staked out in the tunnel. She barely paused for breath. 'And the Major is coming here to get you, *now*.'

'Well, we've seen no sign of him,' said Gigantus. 'And he doesn't stand much chance against all of us on his own.'

'He'll have the other two soldiers with him,' Sheba said. 'They'll probably be here any minute.'

'Right, that's it, I'm off,' said Pyewacket. He made to run for the yard gate, but Gigantus caught hold of his collar.

'None of us is going anywhere,' the big man said. 'At least not until tonight, when we put a stop to this woman's plans once and for all. If this Major and his friends want a fight, they're welcome to one.'

'But they're going to *kill* you!' Sheba wanted to give Gigantus a shake, but knew it would be like a flea trying to budge a mountain.

'Maybe we should leave,' said Mama Rat. 'We could use the time to get to Hyde Park and stop Mrs Crowley in the act.'

'That sounds like a *brilliant* idea,' said Pyewacket.

Sister Moon agreed, and to Sheba's relief Gigantus reluctantly nodded. They all headed back into the house to grab what they might need.

Just as they were making their final preparations, a hideous moan came from the front room. Plumpscuttle. He was finally coming round.

The troupe poked their heads round the door of the parlour.

'Is he dying?' Pyewacket whispered, sounding a little hopeful.

Plumpscuttle groaned loudly and tried to sit up, then quickly lay back down. He looked as though an entire ton of fireworks had just gone off in his head. Underneath the dried blood and bruises, his skin was white and clammy. He tried to speak, but the effort made him pass out again.

'What's wrong with him?' Gigantus asked. He didn't sound very sympathetic.

'It looks like he's concussed,' said Mama Rat. 'Maybe a broken rib or something. Those thugs did a good job on him.'

'About time someone did,' Gigantus said. He looked as though he wished it had been him.

'I think we ought to take him to hospital, you know.' Mama Rat was checking his pulse. 'He should be seen by a doctor. And besides, we can't just leave him here if a bunch of cut-throats are about to come calling.'

'They've already beaten him up once,' said Pyewacket. 'They might not want to bother again.'

'The London Hospital is nearby,' Sister Moon suggested. 'Maybe Gigantus could take him and meet us back here?'

Sheba was about to object, but Gigantus was already reaching to pick Plumpscuttle up.

'Don't worry, Sheba,' said Gigantus. 'I'm just dropping him off. I'll be back before you know it.'

*

The minutes that Gigantus was missing seemed to crawl past like hours. Sheba paced the floorboards of the front room, while the others stood about, fidgeting. *This is a mistake*, she thought. *We should have gone while we had the chance.* But if they had left Plumpscuttle here, then he would surely have been killed in their place. He was a horrid bully, but did he really deserve that? *Of course not*, Sheba told herself. *Nobody does, not even a greedy rogue who treats us like cattle.*

'Hurry up, hurry *up*,' she muttered under her breath.

'I'm sure he's going as fast as he can, dearie,' said Mama Rat.

Sheba was about to say it wasn't fast enough, when there was a bang at the front door, hard enough to shake splinters from the wood.

'It's the Major!' she cried. 'He's here! I *knew* this

would happen . . . what are we going to do without Gigantus?'

'We can manage,' said Mama Rat. 'I've been in tighter scrapes than this before.'

'Quick,' said Sister Moon. 'Upstairs.'

Sheba ran up the steps as fast as her little feet would go. Sister Moon, Mama Rat and her darlings were close behind. Pyewacket had gone the other way, dashing through the kitchen. They burst into the bedroom, ran across to the window and looked out into the yard.

A man with a neckerchief covering his mouth was trying to slip silently through the gate. Sheba recognised him as one of the escaped soldiers. He was carrying a rusty meat cleaver that looked as though it had been stolen from a very unhygienic butcher. The weapon had a strange effect on Raggety and Flossy. The big horse began to make a low growling sound, like a tiger, and Flossy actually leaped right out of the stall and butted the intruder with both of his fuzzy heads.

'Flossy, no!' Sheba called, but her voice was lost in the sound of his terrified bleating.

The soldier, after a moment's shock at seeing an animal with two heads, began to swing his cleaver at the little lamb.

Sheba screwed her eyes shut and turned away, listening for the hideous sound of Flossy being chunked into chops. It didn't come. Instead she heard the creak of the kitchen window opening. The soldier was so intent on killing Flossy that he missed seeing Pyewacket creep through the open window and drop down into Raggety's stall.

Sheba opened her eyes again to see Pyewacket quietly unbolt the stall door and clamber onto Raggety's back. If the soldier looked up and saw him now, there would be imp sausages on the menu, as well as lamb chops.

Raggety found city life very dull. He spent most of the time idly chewing straw and coughing through the cloying smoke and fog. Now his gate was open. Any chance to get out of his stall and stretch his massive legs was welcome, and if he got to attack someone in the process, so much the better. Especially if they were just about to hurt his little stable companion, Flossy.

The soldier had just taken a mighty swipe at the lamb, missing him completely, and was readying himself to boot Flossy across the yard. His expression quickly changed to one of horror as he got a close view of a very large horse raising its hind legs for the mother of all kicks.

Before he could blink, Raggety smashed both hooves into his chest. The blow sent the soldier clear off his feet, across the yard and through the door of the rickety privy. It was not the sturdiest of buildings. The soldier crashed straight through the seat and into the brimming pit below.[xxviii] There was a cry of pain, followed by another of utter disgust and then silence.

'Well done, Raggety!' shouted Sheba from the bedroom window.

'Yes! You beauty!' cried Pyewacket, and he slapped Raggety on the rump.

This was a mistake.

The horse had seen the tempting street beyond the open gate. He knew that out there somewhere were lanes and pastures full of sweet clover, just like the ones he visited in the summer. In a split second he was through the gate and off, with Pyewacket clinging to his back and screaming, 'Not that way, you mangy nag! Turn around! Turn around!'

As the sound of Pyewacket's howling faded, the front door rocked with another mighty bang. The Major? Or another of his soldiers? Perhaps both together?

Quickly, Sheba scurried to the top of the stairs, looking down to the room below. Mama Rat moved to the empty rats' box, flicking open a secret panel in the bottom. She drew out her long-barrelled flintlock. Seeing this reminded Sheba of Spindlecrank's pistol, and she fished it from the pocket of her sodden cloak. She checked it to make sure it was wound and not too damp, then glanced over her shoulder to see Sister Moon drawing her knives. The look on her face was cold and deadly. They all held their breath as they heard the door squeak open.

Time seemed to stand still. Sheba imagined someone large and violent hovering just outside, preparing to charge in.

Which was exactly what happened next.

The soldier with the eye patch stormed through, roaring a battle cry and waving a wooden club. He took the stairs three at a time, bellowing all the way – right into the path of Sheba's pistol. There was a small *twang* as she fired. The little dart hit him square between the eyes. He stopped. *Thank goodness it still works*, thought Sheba.

The man swayed on the steps for a moment. Then the flesh of his face began to bubble like a pot of pea soup as scores of boils erupted all over his skin. Waving his hands and wailing, he tumbled back down the stairs, then struggled to his feet and sprinted out of the front door and down the road.

'Good shooting, Sheba,' said Sister Moon, behind her.

Sheba was just about to allow herself a sigh of relief, when she saw – stepping through the doorway, sword drawn – the Major himself.

He turned his one-eyed gaze up the stairs, catching sight of Sheba where she crouched on the top step. His face twisted in surprise for a moment, before returning to its normal expression. That of someone about to slaughter you and everyone you ever cared about.

Sheba dodged back out of sight but it was too late.

'I see you escaped the tunnel,' he called as he walked slowly up the stairs.

Thud. Thud.

'Impressive. But you really are a stupid girl. You should have used your freedom to get as far away from this house as possible. Everyone in it is about to die most horribly.'

'I thought you were a soldier!' Sheba called back. 'Aren't you supposed to protect people?'

Instead of the sudden rush of guilt Sheba was hoping for, the Major just laughed. 'My days protecting your kind are done. Now I serve only myself.'

Thud. Thud.

Sheba, desperate, looked towards Sister Moon. Her friend reached into one of her coat pockets and pulled out a cloth bag, which she threw to Sheba. Inside were metal ball bearings. *What am I supposed to do with these?* she thought. *Challenge him to a game of marbles?*

Sister Moon mimed tipping the bag, before raising her knives again and moving into a fighting crouch, legs bent, poised and ready to spring.

Metal balls underfoot. Slipping. Tripping. Of course.

Sheba emptied the entire contents of the bag down the steps.

Thud. Th . . .

There was a sudden scrambling sound, followed by a loud curse and a series of crashes. Peering over the banister, Sheba saw the Major land in a crumpled heap at the bottom.

'He's down!' she cried. But the celebration didn't last long. It was rudely interrupted by a waft of the most repulsive stink.

Charging in from the kitchen was the first soldier. Somehow he had managed to climb out of the privy hole. But only after getting a thorough coating of its contents.

Sheba watched, helpless with horror, as the Major clambered to his feet and the pair of them started up the stairs, the soldier leading. He seemed to have lost his cleaver in the toilet, but his fists looked dangerous enough.

Sheba raised her shaky hands and fired her pistol again. But nerves spoilt her aim this time, and the dart thudded into the wall, just past the first man's shoulder. She frantically tried to wind the pistol for another shot. There was a twang and a crunch as a cog jammed. The gun was now useless.

Throwing it to one side, she felt fear and anger rippling under her skin. Who needed a gun when your body was a weapon? Her muscles bunched and wriggled, stretching themselves into new, more deadly shapes. Her sharp teeth gnashed, her claws itched to scratch and slash. The animal urge to protect her home took over.

With a snarling scream, she ran headlong at the soldier.

The last thing she remembered was the awful stench as the man's fist swung towards her. She was smacked clear across the bedroom, hit the far wall and slid to the bottom in a heap.

Fat lot of use I was, she thought. She watched the rest of the attack in fuzzy slow motion – almost as if she were having a bad dream.

Far from being pointless, Sheba's act had distracted the soldier for an instant, allowing Mama Rat to step up. She pointed her pistol at the man, but before she could shoot, her rats burst out from the pockets of her coat and swarmed up his body and onto his face. In a frenzy of scratching claws and nipping teeth they began to chew his nose and ears. Howling in pain and terror, and trying to grab at the writhing, slippery rodents, he turned and pounded down the stairs past the Major, and out of the house.

The Major didn't even flinch. Mama Rat levelled her pistol at his face as he reached the top of the stairs, but wasn't quick enough. He moved with frightening speed, grabbing a throwing knife from his belt and flipping it through the air, too fast for Sister Moon to intercept. It thudded into Mama Rat's shoulder.

Sheba and Sister Moon cried out as the woman and her pistol clattered to the floor.

The Major stepped into the bedroom, raising his sabre and smiling.

With a furious yell, Sister Moon launched herself at him, and they began to fight.

It was like watching a dance. A dangerous, deadly ballet.

Sister Moon moved with superhuman speed, lashing out with her twin knives faster than the eye could follow. Her blades clashed with the Major's sabre over and over, rat-a-tat-tat, striking sparks that reflected in her dark glasses.

The Major countered with the confidence and skill of a trained soldier. By simple, quick twists of his wrist, he managed to deflect most of Moon's blows, blocking her attacks and forcing her back, pushing her into a position where he could strike.

And when it came, it was like a cobra lashing out. His sabre flashed across the spot where Moon's head had just been. If it wasn't for her lightning reflexes, the sword would have sliced through her neck. As it was, her top hat was knocked off, falling to the floor in two pieces.

'I loved that hat,' she said, teeth clenched. She doubled the speed of her attacks, hacking at the Major like a demon, ribbons of black hair whirling as she struck.

Now it was Major Kapoor's turn to be forced back. More and more of Moon's blows slipped through his guard, opening up slices in his coat, carving scratches on his face and neck.

Finally, one whistling slash chopped through the leather thong that held his patch in place. It fell away, revealing a ruin of withered, lifeless flesh. His left eye socket was a puckered slit; the side of his mouth had pulled back, showing the tendons of his jaw and the blackened gums inside.

As Sister Moon froze in horror, the Major struck, his sword tip nicking Moon's left forearm, sending a tiny splatter of blood across her cheek. She jumped back from the stairwell, gasping. It was the first time anyone had managed to land a blow on her.

The Major laughed at her shocked expression. His shrivelled face beamed with triumph.

'I am going to gut you,' he whispered, 'then finish off the hairy girl and the rat woman. You'll never meddle in anyone's business again.'

'Not if I have anything to do with it,' came a deep, furious voice from the front door.

It was Gigantus.

Sheba would have cheered if she had been able to move her mouth.

The Major span to meet the new threat, just in time to see Gigantus's right fist, which was travelling towards his face at about a hundred miles an hour. It slammed into his mouth with a tooth-shattering crunch, followed by the sound of his jaw breaking in several places at once. He staggered back into the room, past the bodies of Mama Rat and Sheba, then Gigantus grabbed him by the collar and threw him through the bedroom window and out into the yard. He left a brief, shining arc of smashed glass and blood behind him, and then landed on the packed mud with a solid thump.

Gigantus and Moon stood for a moment, looking at each other and the shattered mess around them, stunned by how close they had come to disaster.

And then Mama Rat groaned and they both rushed to her side.

CHAPTER SEVENTEEN

In which Sheba finally visits the Great Exhibition.

'Hold still.'

Sister Moon was trying to sew up the wound in Mama Rat's shoulder. Major Kapoor's knife had cut deep, but luckily only into the muscle. Mama sat with her teeth gritted and her face pale. Sheba held her hand.

'Did anyone see where the little idiot went?' Gigantus asked. He was downstairs by the broken front door, looking up and down the street for Pyewacket. When nobody answered he shut the door, then tutted as it swung open again. 'We're going to need a new lock.'

'And a new bedroom window,' said Sister Moon. 'Plumpscuttle will go mad.'

'Let's hope he stays in hospital for a while, then,' muttered Gigantus.

Sheba looked around the battered house. There was blood and broken glass all over the floor. The wall by the stairs had been chopped and sliced by Sister Moon and the Major. *The Major* . . .

Still feeling shaky, she got to her feet and tottered upstairs to the smashed window. Being careful to avoid the broken glass around the edges, she looked down into the yard. There was nothing there. He was gone.

She dashed down the stairs, calling to Gigantus, and ran into the yard. There was a large bloodstained spatter where the Major must have landed, dotted with the twinkle of glass shards. Smaller puddles of red led through the open side gate, where they soon mingled with the muck and cobbles of Brick Lane, trampled into smudges by the crowds.

'I shouldn't worry,' said Gigantus from behind her. 'He's in no fit state to hurt anyone after what I did to him. He'll be crawling into a hole somewhere, licking his wounds.'

Sheba hoped Gigantus was right. But even as he shut and bolted the gate, she couldn't help feeling that they hadn't seen the last of Major Kapoor.

*

It was a few hours before Pyewacket turned up. By then Mama Rat was properly bandaged and drinking tea, while Sheba had calmed Flossy down after his ordeal, soaked herself in a hot bath and put on some clean clothes. Her whole body was a mass of bruises and scrapes, and she felt as though she could sleep for a week. She was just telling the others what had happened to her in the tunnel again, when there was a pounding at the door.

With the lock still broken, it swung wide to reveal a group of angry-looking costermongers. They were leading a grumpy, glaring shire horse, with a fuming Pyewacket on its back.

'Is this your blooming 'orse?' one said. He looked as though he wanted to thump someone. At least until

Gigantus stood up and stomped over to the door.

'Yes,' said Gigantus. 'What of it?'

'Oh, nothing, sir.' The costermonger took off his hat and cowered. 'We just thought you'd like 'im back.'

Gigantus took the reins, while the men hurried back along Brick Lane.

Pyewacket called after them. 'I *told* you my friend was bigger than you!'

'Watch who you're calling friend, imp,' said Gigantus. But Sheba could tell he was secretly relieved to see Pyewacket was back safe and sound.

It turned out that Raggety had galloped straight to the nearest market and eaten almost an entire stall of flowers before the men had managed to drag him away. They would have called the police, had one of them not recognised Pyewacket from Plumpscuttle's sideshow.

'They said they were going to give me a good hiding,' he said, once Sheba had coaxed Raggety back in his stall with more sugar. 'So I told them I hadn't changed my undercrackers in three years.'

'What now, then?' Mama Rat asked.

There was a long pause as everyone considered their options.

'We know she's going to rob the Great Exhibition tonight,' said Sheba. 'Maybe we could tell the police: get them to arrest her?'

Gigantus shook his craggy head. 'No policeman in his right mind is going to believe a story like that. Especially when it comes from a bunch like us.'

'I know,' said Pyewacket. 'How about we just forget the whole thing? It was fun while it lasted, but nearly being killed more than once in a day is just being greedy.'

Mama Rat pretended she hadn't heard him. 'Well, we don't know where this professor has taken the children – or why he wants them. But it's bound to be something horrid. The only lead we have is the Exhibition. You did say you wanted to see it, Sheba.'

Sheba nodded, remembering how exotic it had sounded when she read about it in the paper. But that was before she'd had to break into the place to thwart an evil mastermind.

*

The hansom cab screeched to a halt at Hyde Park Corner. Sparks had been flying from the left axle all the way from Whitechapel, where Gigantus's weight had been forcing the suspension down onto bare metal. As its strange cargo poured out of the door, the cab sprang back upright with such force, the cabbie nearly shot off his perch at the front.

'That's two shillings!' he shouted. 'Not including the damage you've done to me blooming axle!'

One of the passengers flung a handful of copper pennies up at him as the odd group ran off toward Hyde Park.

'Oi! This isn't enough!' the cabbie yelled after them, but his passengers were already out of earshot.

'This way,' Gigantus panted as he ran. 'It's before midnight, so the gates are still open, even if the Exhibition is closed.'

There were several small groups of people walking in and out of the park. At the sight of the hulking man charging towards them like a bull elephant, they scattered in all directions.

'Where's the Exhibition?' asked Sheba. She'd been expecting an enormous glass palace filling the horizon: spires jutting skyward and glinting in the starlight. All she could see now were trees and bushes.

'This way,' said Gigantus. 'Down Rotten Row.'[xxix] He pointed to a long, straight, sandy track that ran into the park. It was lined with trees and benches, most occupied by huddles of ragged women and children.

They all set off down the track at a jog. Sheba was impatient to get to the Crystal Palace as quickly as possible, but Mama Rat was already breathing hard. Sister Moon and Pyewacket loped easily beside her, and from the bushes nearby she could hear rustling and scurrying that could only be the rats. Her own legs were beginning to ache when they came to a little bridge.

'We'd better get off the road now,' said Sister Moon. 'There are soldiers about.'

Up ahead, a small patrol was marching behind their sergeant. All had long rifles with bayonets fixed to the ends. The troupe quickly scurried behind the nearest bush.

'You think that's bad,' whispered Gigantus. 'There's a whole flipping barracks full of them just over the road.'

But Sheba didn't really hear him. She was looking past the soldiers, to where a wide lake stretched off into the park. The stars were reflected in its clear surface. Compared to the murky, crowded chaos of the Thames, it looked so peaceful and serene.

'Strike me down with a feather,' said Pyewacket, who was crouching next to her.

'I know,' said Sheba. 'Beautiful, isn't it.'

'Not the Serpentine, you plum! That!'

When Sheba saw what he meant, her mouth fell open.

The Crystal Palace.

It wasn't the fairytale castle she had imagined. It was far more spectacular than that.

There were no turrets or towers or drawbridges. In fact, it looked more like an enormous wedding cake than a palace. Tiers of glass and metal were stacked up into the sky and topped off with a gigantic arch. It was wider, taller, grander than any building Sheba had seen . . . than any she had even imagined.

And the entire thing was transparent, glittering in the moonlight like diamond. Thousands upon

thousands of window panes, somehow supporting each other without smashing into shards. The mechanics of it were astounding.

'It's . . . it's . . .' she tried to say, but words failed her.

'The biggest greenhouse in the world?' said Pyewacket. 'A window cleaner's worst nightmare?'

They all stared as the glow of gas lamps and moonlight played across the expanse of shining glass before them. It was so magnificent, they forgot for a moment why they were there.

'Well, how are we going to get in?' Pyewacket said at last. 'We can't fly up to the roof, and if we try and smash in through the wall, we'll be full of lead before we can blink.'

From where they hid they could see more patrols of guards marching past. There were also two large police lodges between the palace and the park's edge.

'That's an entrance, there,' said Gigantus, pointing to a series of doors at the east end of the building, which was closest to them. But they looked securely locked, and a policeman was standing sentry.

'If we can get to the back wall, I can cut a way

in,' said Sister Moon.

'What with?' Sheba looked at Moon's knives. Surely they weren't that sharp?

'This,' said Sister Moon. She pulled a stick from her coat pocket, wrapped around with a length of string. 'It's got a small diamond in the end. For cutting glass.'

'Why on earth have you got one of those?' Pyewacket asked. 'Sneak into posh greenhouses often, do you?'

'It's from when I lived with my father,' Moon said, frowning. 'Housebreaking was just one of the jobs he used me for.'

Sheba sensed a whole untold story there, but now was not the time. 'Then what we need is a diversion,' she said.

There was a brief silence, in which all eyes turned to Pyewacket.

'Oh no,' he said. 'Don't even look at me. I've been used as bait once already. It's someone else's turn now.'

'Maybe one of us could run down to the far end,' said Sheba. 'Throw a stone through the glass, draw the soldiers' attention . . . Wait a minute! What are they doing?'

The five rats had scurried out of the bush and were dashing towards one of the police lodges.

'Come back!' Mama Rat hissed after them.

'I think,' said Sheba, 'that they're giving us our diversion.'

The scampering cluster of black shadows disappeared into the lodge. Everyone held their breath and Sheba felt Mama Rat squeezing her arm. Moments later, there was a piercing scream and the sound of a gunshot.

Within seconds soldiers and policemen from all over the park were running towards the source of the noise.

'Now!' hissed Sheba. 'Quickly!'

They sprinted across the grass to the rear of the Crystal Palace, just around the corner from the east entrance. Sister Moon had the diamond cutter ready.

Working quickly, she slapped one end of the string against the glass wall. A ball of sticky rubber held it in place. Next she stretched out the string and then pressed the stick against the glass. Using the stuck piece as an anchor, she dragged it around in a wide circle, and then pulled. A perfectly round section of glass popped out from the wall with a soft grinding sound.

'There we go,' she said, smiling. 'Now get in, quickly!'

Not needing to be told twice, they all clambered through, emerging into a dark, silent room. Sister Moon rested the glass back against the wall. Hopefully no one would spot the hole.

'Well, we're in,' said Gigantus. 'Where's this diamond, then?'

Sheba cast her mind back to the articles she had once read in that other, far more boring life. 'I think it's in the centre. Next to the big fountain.'

They took a moment to look around. In the darkness, it seemed as though the room was full of hulking metal monsters with jutting spikes and blades. They were all reminded of the mechanical crab, and Gigantus looked ready to pound the nearest one into scrap.

'Relax,' said Sister Moon, using her night sight to read a plaque. 'They're just farm machines.

From America.'

They were about to head out of the room when something scrabbled at the glass behind them.

They turned as one, expecting to see a squad of soldiers with rifles levelled straight at them.

Instead a writhing bundle of black fur heaved its way up and through the hole Sister Moon had cut. It separated into five squeaking rats.

Mama Rat bent down to cuddle them all with a squeal of joy. 'You naughty little ratties!' she whispered. 'Don't you dare run off like that again!'

Sheba whispered a thank you to the brave rats and then led everyone out of the room and into the main corridor, which stretched all the way down the east wing.

The inside of the Great Exhibition was just as impressive as the exterior. Tall columns of iron stretched up to the panels of the glass ceiling. Potted plants and small trees surrounded them, and there were thick carpets, drapes and banners everywhere. Exhibits lined the walkway on both sides. Sheba could see statues of tigers, horses and dragons, and people in costumes from all ages.

'This way to the diamond!' Sheba said, spotting a sign in the dim light. 'Hurry!'

They began to dash along the corridor, zipping past exhibits in a blur. Almost at the centre, they were stopped by Pyewacket shouting.

'Look at this! Look at this!'

'If you've stopped us to gawk—' began Gigantus, but saw he was pointing at an object in what looked like an enormous birdcage, topped with a crown. Inside it, on a velvet cushion, was a diamond the size of a fist. The plaque beneath read 'The Koh-i-noor, Mountain of Light'. In the darkness of the empty Exhibition it barely gave a twinkle. It could have just been an expensive lump of glass.[xxx]

'It's the diamond!' Sheba whispered. 'But why hasn't it been taken?'

Sister Moon drew her knives and looked around the shadows of the central court. The fountains were still, the main doors locked and barred. 'Are we early?' she suggested. 'Maybe Mrs Crowley isn't here yet?'

'Are you sure she said it was tonight, Sheba?' Mama Rat asked.

'I'm certain,' said Sheba.

'Unless that's what she wanted you to think,' said Sister Moon.

'You mean we've just broken into the most famous building in England for nothing?' Pyewacket said. He stared around, wide-eyed, waiting for some kind of trap to be sprung. But there was nothing except the dark, the stillness and the blank stares of statues.

The silence was long and uncomfortable. Sheba could feel everyone's eyes burning into her.

'I was *sure* it was the diamond,' she said, feeling helpless. 'Although she did laugh when I said it. But what else could she be after?'

'Well, we'd better do something soon, or a guard's going to come past and catch us standing here, and then we'll be on display. At the nearest prison,' Pyewacket whispered.

Sheba nodded, heartbroken. She had been expecting to charge in and find Mrs Crowley, complete with all the mudlarks, in the act of stealing the diamond. *As if it was ever going to be that easy.*

'She must be here somewhere,' said Sister Moon, trying to be positive.

'I suggest we split up,' said Mama Rat, 'or we're never going to find her. And it's only a matter of time before someone spots the hole we cut. Then we've had it.'

'Pyewacket and I can take the top galleries,' said Sister Moon.

'I'll go this way, then,' said Mama Rat. 'Gigantus, you head left. Sheba: straight ahead. If anyone spots her . . . give a signal.'

Sister Moon nodded and scrambled up one of the columns to the first floor. Pyewacket copied her on the opposite side. Sheba marvelled at how they climbed: Pyewacket as naturally as an ape, Sister Moon silent and graceful. She couldn't even see the tiny footholds they used.

Gigantus clomped off at a jog, as did Mama and her rats.

That just left Sheba, standing in the dark, empty atrium, feeling very small, very alone.

Here goes, she thought. She took a step forward and then stopped, nostrils twitching.

There were many new and strange aromas inside the palace: machine oil, minerals, freshly varnished wood and foreign spices. But underneath them all was a hint of something else. A scent she'd come across before, and recently.

Mrs Crowley. She was here.

Taking a deep breath, Sheba followed her nose.

*

The scent was coming from higher up, weaving down from the galleries on the first floor. An invisible trail, like a thread floating in the air.

Sheba tiptoed past the fountain and up the stairs. They led to a set of open doors. The gold banner above it said *India*.

There was a hint of moonlight shining through the glass roof overhead. Strange silhouettes loomed everywhere as Sheba stood in the doorway of the room, frozen at the sight of a colossal, tusked monster, rearing up to the ceiling. Her hands shot to her mouth, holding back a scream, before she realised it was an elephant. A stuffed one, draped with embroidered silk and bearing a howdah large enough to house a small family. She stood still, trying to control her breathing, before padding into the room.

All around her were fabulous objects, decorated in the intricate and ornate Indian style. In the dim light she made out thrones and a beautiful tent crammed with carpets and cushions. There were spices, rocks and plants; a sample of everything the Indian soil could produce. The rich mix of new scents made Sheba's head spin. And beneath that was the same nagging feeling she'd had when she met Mrs Crowley . . . saw the clipper . . . heard Major Kapoor's accent. She had definitely smelled something in here before. Nose twitching, she followed the trail to a small plant in an earthen pot. It had a powerful, unmistakable aroma, coming from its small white flowers. Flowers like the carved ones on her ebony box. They were labelled as jasmine, a native Indian plant. She must have come across them some time in her unknown past. But how? She was a furry little orphan from a tatty seaside town. What did she know of Indian flowers?

As if in answer, that fragment of a memory came back, stronger than ever before.

She is running through a house, her tiny, bare feet slap-slap-slapping against cool marble. Patches of scorching sunlight shine through tall open windows. She turns corner after corner, finally emerging into a courtyard: trickling water, wide blue sky above.

A figure sits by the pond, beckoning her. White skirts, a parasol. And she can smell the jasmine . . .

'Mama?'

No! Not here! Not now . . . Pressing her hand over her mouth, Sheba dashed out of the Indian room.

She paused at the bottom of a flight of stairs, taking a moment to calm herself. Had that been a real memory? Or was it just a mirage? An illusion her brain had stitched together out of everything she wanted so badly . . .

Away from the smell of jasmine, her head began to clear. There would be time to puzzle this out, she told herself. But she needed to find Mrs Crowley first. Her scent was still there, suspended in the air like a memory. Sheba began to follow it again.

She ran past a gallery full of farming equipment, another dedicated to different types of cutlery, and a room full of what looked like surgical implements.

Now the scent was stronger still, accompanied by a grinding noise from up ahead. It was a metallic sound, as if something was being cut. Her first thought was the bars of the Koh-i-noor's birdcage, but that was far behind her now, back in the central court.

She took the clockwork pistol out from her cape. She had tried to unjam it during their ride in the cab, but there hadn't been a chance to test it. She prayed it would work when she needed it to.

The room from which the noise came was labelled *Philosophical Instruments.* Mrs Crowley's scent was strong now. She was definitely in that room, and Sheba could smell neither the mudlarks nor the professor. There was a dim glow inside. A lantern? And the metallic sawing was louder than ever.

Sheba paused outside the doorway, as if an invisible barrier blocked her path. Should she go and get the others? But what if Mrs Crowley already had what she needed? She might be gone by the time Sheba got back.

There was no time for making a plan. She gathered all her courage and stepped through the door, pistol raised.

The room was lined with display cases, all of them holding bundles of tubes, pipes, cogs, wires, dials and handles that looked immensely complicated. They could have been machines for making tea, shaving your eyebrows or summoning leprechauns for all Sheba knew. Standing in the centre of the room, holding a shuttered lantern[xxxi], was a slender figure, dressed all in black.

Gone were the skirts, the bodice and the veil, but it was still unmistakably Mrs Crowley. She now wore trousers and a shirt with some kind of harness over the top. The bottom half of her face was covered by a neckerchief, tied behind her head like a highwayman, and her eyes were hidden beneath the lenses of a pair of goggles. Her hair was pulled back in a tight bun and she was standing next to an exhibit that was clearly the centrepiece of the room. Unlike the others, it had been given its own cage, which Mrs Crowley was trying to break into. In her hands was a hacksaw, and the ground around her was littered with cut iron bars.

She looked up as Sheba entered. The pale skin of her forehead wrinkled in a frown.

'You really are irritatingly persistent, aren't you?' she said.

'Stop what you're doing,' said Sheba. She couldn't quite keep her voice from shaking. 'Stop right now, or I'll shoot.'

'If you shoot me with your toy gun – presuming you actually hit me, that is – then you'll never find that scrawny girl you're looking for.' Sheba knew she was right. Even though she itched to pull the trigger, finding Till was more important.

'Besides,' Mrs Crowley continued, 'there is another very good reason why you shouldn't shoot me.'

'I can't think of one.' Sheba kept the pistol aimed between Mrs Crowley's eyes, ready to fire.

'Have you ever wondered about your parents, Sheba? Has it ever puzzled you how you ended up a strange little orphan, unwanted and alone?'

Sheba's hands began to shake. The pistol muzzle jittered. 'You don't know anything about me.' The woman was bluffing; lying again like she had about her kidnapped son.

'That's not entirely true,' Mrs Crowley said. 'In fact, I know quite a bit. Would you like to hear it?'

'You're lying,' said Sheba. The tremble had spread to her voice. 'You've only met me twice before.'

'That was more than enough, my dear. It took me a while to make the connection, but how many girls like you can there be in the world? A simple investigation proved my suspicions correct.'

'You don't know me!' Sheba shouted. 'If you did, you wouldn't have ordered your Major to kill me!'

'I did, didn't I?' The woman raised a finger to her hidden lips as if it had been an innocent mistake. 'I must apologise. In hindsight, that was an error of judgement. I should have killed you myself.'

'You lied about your son, and you're lying now. You're nothing but an evil, child-stealing hag!' Sheba felt her teeth gnash and her eyes blaze as the fur stood out all over her face.

'I'm surprised you don't remember me, actually. Not my face, of course, but my voice at least. What about the jasmine garden? The ornamental ponds? Or perhaps those long, white corridors you used to run up and down.'

Suddenly the room seemed very small and airless. Sheba's chest squeezed tight, making it hard for her to breathe. Her heart seemed to pound in her ears, and the only thing she could do was open her mouth and croak, 'No . . .'

'So, you *do* remember. And how about your dear governess? The poor young woman dragged from her home country, halfway across the world, to some cursed Indian hellhole?'

'You?' Sheba managed to say. She had no memory of this woman, not even the faintest glimmer. But she knew about the white house, about the jasmine. And that hint of Mrs Crowley's scent that was so familiar . . . Could Sheba's nose recall what the rest of her brain had lost?

'Yes, me. Hard to believe, isn't it? I wanted to study science, like my brother, but as a mere woman I wasn't allowed.[xxxii] Instead I had to become a glorified slave, running around at the bidding of your mother and trying to teach her ungrateful brat how to read . . .'

'Mama . . .' Sheba's lip began to tremble. All those years of dreaming about her, and this woman might actually know where she was.

'Where is she?' Mrs Crowley read her mind. 'Who knows now? When you began to change . . .

the shock nearly killed her. She was bedridden for months, and then one night she snatched you and left. The last I heard, she had boarded a clipper for England. Perhaps she thought the Indian air might have caused it. Perhaps she wanted to hide you away in that crumbling hole of a house I've been living in. Maybe she wanted to escape your father. God knows she had reasons enough. She must have died on the journey home, leaving you an orphan. And now an exhibit in a tawdry carnival, of all things. How shameful.'

India, the ship, the memories, it all seemed to fit.

'Father?' Sheba managed to say, even as her legs buckled and she fell to the floor.

'I shouldn't spare a thought for him,' said Mrs Crowley. 'The brute wanted you locked away from the moment you started sprouting hair. After you and your mother left he was racked with grief. And then he caught the wasting disease. The same one that . . . Well, let's just say that his end was far from pleasant. At least it allowed me to steal your family fortune. Even if it was just a few measly diamonds.'

'They're dead.' Sheba felt hot tears run down her cheeks. 'They're both dead.' Her worst fears had proved true. She really was alone in the world. Utterly alone.

'Why cry about it?' Mrs Crowley sounded disgusted. 'You never even knew them. Not really. You were always a disgrace to them.'

Sheba didn't want to believe that was true. Why would her mother run away with her if she couldn't stand her? But part of what Mrs Crowley said was right. Crying over the loss of something you never knew was stupid. Instead, she should be fighting for what she *did* have. This heartless criminal had kidnapped the only normal friend Sheba had ever known. Thinking of Till stopped her tears. She still didn't know where the mudlarks were, or what the woman intended to do with them. Somehow, she had to find out.

She watched as Mrs Crowley reached inside the display case and lifted out a box-like contraption. It had loops of coiled wire jutting from the top, rods and cables poking out all over, and brass buttons and dials set into the mahogany casing.

That thing? Sheba thought. *That's what she's been after?*

Mrs Crowley placed the device in a black canvas bag.

'Curious, are we? Wondering why it wasn't the diamond?'

'No,' Sheba said, a fraction too quickly. 'I just need to know what's been stolen when I scream for the police.'

Mrs Crowley gave a sharp, bitter laugh. 'If you must know, it is Mr Faraday's electromagnetic impulse generator. Not that I expect you to understand its importance.' She heaved the bag onto her back and began clipping it to her harness. She watched Sheba closely the whole time. 'Given up on shooting me then, have you?'

Sheba looked at the pistol in her hand. She could fire and stop her now . . . but then she would never find Till and the others. The choice was simple. 'I . . . I can't.'

'Thought as much.' Mrs Crowley took a step backwards. Sheba could see a circular hole cut in the glass behind her, much like the one Sister

Moon had made.

She climbed the wall, Sheba realised. *Like a giant, poisonous spider.*

'You won't escape, you know,' Sheba said. 'There are hundreds of soldiers and policemen out there.'

'Yes, but they're all going to be busy.' Mrs Crowley took a pocket watch from her belt and flipped it open. 'Right about *now.*'

From somewhere deep inside the Crystal Palace came a thunderous bang, followed by the sound of hundreds of panes of glass exploding. The walls around them shook violently, setting all the exhibits rattling in their cases.

As Sheba curled on the floor, her first thought was for her friends, that one of them might have been caught by the blast. They might be lying there right now, as razor-sharp shards cascaded down. She had a sudden urge to dash back out of the room to find them all, to make sure they were safe.

But Mrs Crowley was moving again. She picked up a coil of black rope and tied it to the remains of the iron cage she had just dismantled. The other end she threw out of the hole.

'What about the children?' Sheba cried.

Mrs Crowley laughed, and squeezed through the hole in the glass. There she paused, her feet braced on the side of the Crystal Palace.

'If you could only witness what I'm going to do with your precious mudlarks – what I could do for *you* – you wouldn't care less about saving them, believe me. Follow me if you like. If you can.'

Then she slipped out of sight.

Sheba ran to the window and looked down to see her shadowy shape zipping to the ground. Somewhere to her right was the red glow of fire, and hordes of men in army uniform were sprinting towards the Crystal Palace.

There was no time to find her friends and get them to safety. There was only the rope downwards or the pistol in her hand. Chase Mrs Crowley or shoot her. One terrible decision.

Sheba grabbed the rope, put her foot on the edge of the glass, and jumped.

CHAPTER EIGHTEEN

In which foes are faced and battles fought.

Sheba spilled from the bottom of the rope and onto the grass with a thump that jarred every bone in her body. There was chaos everywhere. Smoke poured from a shattered hole at the west end of the Palace. Jagged shards of glass surrounded a roaring blaze, like teeth in a dragon's mouth. Soldiers swarmed, shouting for hoses and water. The night was filled with noise and burning.

She picked herself up and looked around in time to see a dark figure dashing away from the Crystal Palace towards the cover of the trees.

Mrs Crowley.

Sheba sprinted after her.

They ran through the shadows of Hyde Park, back along Rotten Row. Crowds were starting to gather, come to stare at the burning Crystal Palace. Mrs Crowley weaved through them, keeping close to the trees and bushes. Sheba struggled to follow, turning her head every now and then, hoping to spot the others among the throngs of gawkers.

But they were nowhere to be seen.

Near the park gates, Mrs Crowley finally slowed her pace. Sheba had a chance to catch up, although she had to keep straining on tiptoe to spot the woman in the crowds.

Snippets of what she had said kept running through Sheba's mind. *A governess. A mother. A father.* But it was all too big to think about right now. First, she had to find the mudlarks, discover what Mrs Crowley was up to, and then try and come to terms with it all. It would keep.

Finally, Mrs Crowley left the crowds and stepped out onto Hyde Park Corner. A horse-drawn fire engine was edging through the gates, bells clanging. She calmly moved aside, the firemen not realising the very cause of the blaze was standing right next to them.

Sheba watched as Mrs Crowley crossed the road, natural as anything, walking towards a grand white building. When she thought nobody was looking, she slipped around the side.

Still panting for breath after her sprint, Sheba gritted her teeth and pushed through the gathering crowds in pursuit.

Outside the stately white mansion was a sign. *St George's Hospital.* Could the mudlarks be inside? Why would they be in a hospital? Then she remembered Mrs Crowley's brother, the professor. His stink of dead meat and interest in dissecting animals. A cold shiver of fear made her hackles rise.

She tracked Mrs Crowley's scent trail around the side of the mansion and emerged into a maze of much older, smaller buildings. Some were in the process of being demolished, scaffolding covering their sides in rickety cocoons, and the ground in between was covered with piles of bricks and worm-eaten timber.

Sheba spotted Mrs Crowley ducking under a tarpaulin and into one of these derelict buildings.

Pulling her cape tight about her, Sheba followed.

It was dark inside, and filled with strange smells. Decades of dust, damp brick and plaster mingled with a mixture of medical odours. Sheba smelled dried blood, soap and starch; chemicals, disease and chamber pots. All of it was old and faded. A disused hospital, perhaps, Sheba thought. A part of St George's once upon a time? There was a steep, winding staircase in front of her.

Mrs Crowley's footsteps echoed from somewhere above. Sheba saw the woman's shadow moving round and round, the bulging pack jutting out like a hunched back.

She followed up the creaking steps – one, two, three floors – and then walked towards a door that glowed with flickering gaslight. Painted on the wall outside were the words *Operating Theatre*.

Funny place to put on a performance, she thought, but when she peeked around the door she realised it was for a different kind of show entirely.

Mrs Crowley was in the centre of the room. She was unpacking Faraday's generator on a workbench and, standing beside her, as excited as an infant on

Christmas morning, was her brother. Around them were more tables, covered in saws and knives, vials, bottles, tubes and piping. The whole scene was taking place in a lowered pit, surrounded by six or seven tiers of benches, all descending towards the stage space at the bottom.

It *was* a place for watching, Sheba realised. But the performance wasn't a penny gaff show. It was chopping and slicing and hacking. Victorian surgery.[xxxiii]

Sheba began to shake. Her worst fears about why Mrs Crowley and the professor might have brought the mudlarks to a place like this were coming true. Something more vile, more horrific than she could ever have imagined. And that was when she saw them. Bound and gagged at the back of the theatre. All nine children.

Looming over them was another figure. It took Sheba a while to recognise him, as his face and hands were swathed in blood-spotted bandages, but when he looked up at her with that single glaring eye she knew it couldn't be anyone else. Major Kapoor! So much for him not hurting anyone again.

'Come down, girl,' called Mrs Crowley, as if she had always known Sheba was there. 'We are about to begin. And you will find this especially interesting.'

Sheba began to descend the stairs in front of her. The Major watched her all the way. His jaw was oddly lopsided, held in place by a thick bandage surrounding his head. Through gaps in the binding, she saw glimpses of his withered flesh. Ignoring him, Sheba's eyes flicked all around, looking for something, anything that might help her put a stop to this.

'It's splendid, simply beautiful.' The professor was fawning over the generator, rubbing his bony hands over the mahogany casing.

The Major was still gazing fiercely at her. He tried to say something, but with his broken jaw so bandaged, all that came out was, 'Mmng ug ee ooing ere?'

'Hush,' said Mrs Crowley. 'Once I show her what we are about to do, we will have no more silliness, I'm sure. She's a resourceful girl. Perhaps I was wrong, wanting to destroy her. She might even like to become my pupil again. How long until we are ready, brother dearest?'

The professor adjusted a few switches on the generator, then turned the crank handle. Metal discs on the top began to whizz around, and blue crackles of light started jumping between the coils. This made him clap his hands with glee, while Mrs Crowley and the Major flinched. Sheba stared, amazed. It was like watching tamed lightning.

Taking some copper wires from the rest of his apparatus, the professor attached them to the generator. Then he turned to Mrs Crowley and gave a fawning bow. 'We are ready now, sister. We just need the first batch of *ingredients*.'

As if that were some prearranged signal, the Major bent and hoisted up one of the mudlarks. He heaved the wriggling, squealing child towards the operating table. Sheba recognised the scared brown eyes that stared at her above the gagged mouth. It was Till.

'Wait!' Sheba shouted. 'You haven't told me what you're doing yet! What's all this . . . all this *stuff* for?'

She pointed at the professor's table, where the sparking generator was whirring away. Its cables led to a glass crucible on a stand, which was now starting to bubble, letting off a strong chemical stink.

'This, Sheba, is the miracle I was telling you about,' said Mrs Crowley. She took a clay pot from the table and removed the lid to reveal a grey, pulpy cream.

'It doesn't look much like a miracle to me,' said Sheba. The stuff stank – the same graveyard reek that she had smelled on the professor's clothes at the Paradise Street house.

'Haven't you ever despaired at your . . . condition?' Mrs Crowley asked. 'Haven't you ever wished away your cursed differences and dreamed of being normal? I know the Major and I have.'

As Sheba watched, Mrs Crowley reached up and lifted her goggles. Underneath were surprisingly young eyes, elegantly shaped. Her nose was small, slightly upturned, but dainty. She's beautiful, Sheba thought.

But then Mrs Crowley removed the black neckerchief.

From her nose downwards, the features were withered and shrunken. Her lips were gone, exposing jagged teeth hanging by threads in leathery gums. It was the face of someone long dead; a mummified corpse's mouth, like something you would find grinning up at you from an ancient grave. The same shrivelled wreckage that had been hidden behind the Major's patch.

'Pleasant, isn't it?' The distorted mouth gnashed as Mrs Crowley lisped the words. 'A souvenir of my time in India. The very disease that killed your father, and most of those in the hospital we ended up in. Major Kapoor, his friends and I were the lucky ones. If you can call looking like this "luck".'

As Sheba stared in terror, trying not to scream, the woman dipped her fingers into the pot and smeared some of the grey goo onto her cheek. Instantly the withered skin started to change. It became plump, smooth and pale, like the rest of her face. Sheba let out a gasp of amazement. She couldn't believe what she was seeing. It was like some kind of magic.

'Try some,' said Mrs Crowley. 'You and I are very much alike, you see. With this, both of us could be normal. Neither of us need hide ourselves away again. Not ever.' She took hold of Sheba's hand and smeared a dab onto the back.

As Sheba stared, she felt her flesh beginning to tingle. When she rubbed her thumb over it, the hair fell away, revealing soft, pink skin underneath.

It works! Sheba thought. For a few perfect seconds, her mind spun with all the wonderful possibilities. No more carnivals. No more hiding from the world in the shadows of her hood. Being able to walk down the street and talk to people, really talk to them, without them running away screaming.

'But the effects are only temporary,' said Mrs Crowley.

Already her patch of cheek was beginning to wrinkle and wither, and when Sheba looked down she could see minute hairs pushing their way out of her own skin again. Mrs Crowley tied the neckerchief back around her mouth.

'That is why we are here today,' she said. 'My brother has found a way to make the change permanent.'

'Yes,' said the professor, blinking his eyes behind the thick lenses of his spectacles. 'The problem is in the subject material. I discovered that only children's would work, but deceased ones were all I could obtain from the Resurrection Men.'

'The *what*?' Sheba knew 'resurrection' meant returning from the dead, but she couldn't believe there were people who had actually *done* that.

'Bodysnatchers or grave-robbers, you might call them,' the professor explained. 'Most useful for supplying corpses to medical explorers like myself. Anyway, I realised that to make the cream take permanent effect, I would need live tissue to combine with my compound. That, and an electrical charge to activate the cells. To bring them to life, as it were. I tried a range of generating devices of my own design, but I couldn't create a powerful enough current. That is why we required Faraday's engine, here. A spectacular piece of engineering. Truly revolutionary. We had to have it for ourselves, before the Exhibition closed.'

'What *material* are you talking about?' asked Sheba, trying to keep calm. 'What is it you're taking from the children?'

'Why, brains of course!' The professor looked at her as if she were stupid. 'Precisely, tissue from the brain stem. In the correct solution, and with an electrical impulse to get things going, it somehow repairs the body's cells. Makes them "normal" again.'

Sheba suddenly realised she still had some cream on her hand. With a shudder, she wiped it off on her dress.

'But the children,' she said, trying to keep her voice from trembling. 'If you cut their brains out, they'll die!'

'And what of it?' said Mrs Crowley. 'They are only starving urchins. This city couldn't care less about them. Apart from you and your annoying friends, nobody has even remarked that they're gone! We spent all that money on Spindlecrank's machine when we could just as well have wandered up to them in broad daylight and scooped them up in a sack. If only we'd known how little England values her poor.'

The professor picked up a jagged silver saw that looked sharp enough to cut through bone.

'This is just a small sacrifice so that I can go on to achieve much greater things,' said Mrs Crowley. 'And you can join me, free from that hairy curse which has landed you in a degrading sideshow. You should be on your knees, thanking me for this opportunity.'

Sheba looked at the terrified face of Till, strapped to the table.

'No!' she cried. 'Never! You can't do this. It's wrong!'

Before she could reach for her pistol, or run at the professor, she felt a pair of steel-strong hands close about her arms. It was the Major. She hadn't even noticed him get behind her.

'Pity,' said Mrs Crowley. 'Too soft, that's your problem. Just like your pathetic mother.' She looked at the Major, who Sheba could feel growling behind her. 'Let's get on with it. Make her watch this first one,' she said. 'Then you can end her miserable life.'

The Major held Sheba tight as the professor moved closer to Till and lowered the saw to her head. Mrs Crowley stood nearby, holding a metal basin and some kind of scoop.

'We have to be quick,' the professor was saying. 'The tissue must be placed in the charged solution before the cells start to decay.'

His words seemed to echo in Sheba's ears as if she were drifting far away. Suddenly she felt very hot, and it was difficult to breathe. The blood pounded and thrummed in her head; each heartbeat seemed to last a minute, and she realised she was fainting. *Stay awake!* she screamed to herself. *Stay awake and DO something!* But what? What on earth could she do on her own?

The teeth of the saw pressed against Till's forehead. Sheba watched bright drops of blood form as they dug into her tender skin. She saw the professor's goggling eyes, focused on their horrid task. A tiny bead of sweat was creeping down his temple at the speed of a snail.

Sheba felt utterly helpless, and totally alone.

And then a silver flash spiralled across the table. A large hunting knife thudded into the professor's arm, sending teardrops of blood flying outwards, like a red rose unfurling.

It was followed by a bang that made Sheba's ears ring, and Mrs Crowley fell backwards in slow motion, the bowl and scoop she was holding flying up into the air. Sheba's terrified mind couldn't fathom what was happening. All she could do was stare at the professor's arm. At the knife-shaped hunk of steel that stood there, quivering.

How on earth did a flying knife get in here? her addled mind wondered.

A second later she understood and, with that understanding, time sprang back to normal.

She looked up.

Sister Moon perched on one of the wooden benches, drawing her other knife.

Mama Rat stood on the steps, rats clustered about her shoulders, smoking flintlock pistol in her hand.

Behind them came Gigantus, yelling a battle cry, and Pyewacket clinging to his back, face white with terror.

'You're safe!' Sheba grinned, tears of joy in her eyes. 'You're here!'

Behind her, the Major let out a muffled roar. He moved one hand from her shoulder to draw his sword, and Sheba took her chance. She sank her needle-sharp fangs into his other wrist and then, when he let go with a cry of surprise, dashed to the other side of the theatre.

'Save Till!' she shouted at her friends.

Even as the others came hurtling down the steps

to where Sheba stood, the professor was already fleeing the room. Wailing with terror, he paused to snatch the electromagnetic impulse generator from the table, scattering and smashing bottles everywhere in the process, and then scurried out of a narrow side door. Mrs Crowley pulled herself up and followed him, slamming the little door behind her. Mama Rat's shot had hit her side and she clutched it as she ran.

'Get the others!' Sister Moon shouted. 'I'll take the Major!'

The bandaged hulk now had his military sabre drawn. He moved towards Sister Moon as she brandished her knife and moved into a fighting stance. Sheba ran to the door, but found it locked tight. She frantically searched for a keyhole to pick, but Gigantus gently moved her aside.

'Quicker if I break it, I think.'

As the big man started to pound on the door, Sheba turned to watch Sister Moon fight the Major.

The man had looked murderous before, but now he was horrific. The unbandaged flesh of his face was criss-crossed with fresh red cuts from the window glass he had been thrown through. His nose was squashed and crooked, the nostrils caked with dried blood. Patches of his withered skin peeped through his bindings, cracked and flaking. He looked at Sister Moon with a fury hot enough to melt lead, then, with a lung-rending howl, he launched himself at her, his sword whistling back and forth through the air, forcing her further up the stairs to the plate-glass windows at the very back.

As he charged, Moon let him come, opening her guard on purpose. Just as he got within sword range, she placed a foot in the centre of his chest and let herself fall backwards onto the floor. His momentum carried him over her head, and at exactly the right moment she kicked hard with her leg and sent him soaring through the air. The old plate window was directly behind them, and for the second time that day, Major Kapoor flew straight through the glass, smashing it with his face. With a disbelieving wail, he vanished into the foggy night, on his way to the ground at high speed.

Sister Moon rolled to her feet, brushing her long black hair from her face. She poked her head through the hole in the window and saw his body lying on a brick pile, three storeys below.

'*That* was for my hat,' she said.

Sheba cheered, just as Gigantus broke open the door with a final blow. Weapons drawn, they all ran full pelt after Mrs Crowley.

*

Sheba sprinted down the crumbling corridors after the fleeing villains. She saw them turn, heading through an open door to her right, and moments later she skidded through it herself.

She emerged into a wide room, floorboards covered with brick dust and rubble. Crowley and her brother were standing in the far corner, both gripping Faraday's generator and refusing to let go.

'We had an agreement, Euan, you fool!' Mrs Crowley was screaming. 'You can have the machine after you've cured me!'

'But those monsters!' the professor yelled back. 'They will kill us! Look at my arm!'

'Stop right there!' Sheba shouted from the

doorway. She had her pistol out again, and this time there was no hesitation. She fired a shot and the dart pinged across the room to hit the professor right in the middle of his bald head. He instantly froze, clutching the generator in a rigor mortis grip.

'Paralysis dart,' Sheba said, as Gigantus and Mama Rat arrived behind her.

Mrs Crowley let out a scream of fury. With shaking hands, she pulled out a box of matches and fumbled to strike one.

'What's she doing now?' asked Pyewacket. 'Smoking a pipe?'

Sheba looked on, bemused. *Maybe we should try and grab her*, she thought, and made a move across the room, just as Mrs Crowley managed to light a match. She gave Sheba a last hate-filled glance, then threw the flaming stick onto the floor. There was a hissing sound, and a cloud of stinking, sulphurous smoke.

'Gunpowder!' Mama Rat shouted. 'The building is booby-trapped!'

Sheba watched in horror as a trail of fire zipped along the side of the room. She could now see a line of black powder that must have been laid out earlier, just in case the evil woman needed to make an escape. It would probably lead to a keg somewhere; enough explosives to bring the whole building down around them.

She should have been filled with terror. She should have turned and run. Instead she was overcome with a rush of anger. This woman who had destroyed her family, kidnapped Till, hurt her friends – she was about to flee into the night. There was no way Sheba could let that happen. Everyone she had hurt, bullied, terrorised – they deserved better than that. And Sheba now knew she had the power to stop her. Strong and ferocious: that timid little girl from the seaside cage was long gone. Let Mrs Crowley see how she fared against her wolfish side . . .

In her head, Sheba opened the locks that held the beast in place. She slammed wide the door, and instantly began to change.

The fur on her face began to thicken. Her jaw stretched, teeth sliding into spiked points. Her eyes blazed, gleaming and glinting with a hunger as old as the first wild hunt. She dropped onto all fours and snarled, snapping her teeth, brimming with an irresistible urge to howl. *This is it*, she thought. *I've finally become a proper wolf.* She was surprised to find that the thought almost pleased her.

As the gunpowder ignited with a boom that shook the walls and threw the others to the ground, Sheba bounded across the room towards Mrs Crowley.

There was fire and smoke everywhere. The explosion had come from the floor beneath, thrusting jagged floorboards up like splintered mountain ranges. It cracked the walls and sent bricks, slates and chunks of timber raining from the ceiling.

Sheba dodged all these, jinking and swerving across the floor, her wolf limbs like wire springs. Mrs Crowley was at a door in the corner, heaving it open while still trying to drag the generator from her brother's grip. The smoke in front of her parted, and the snarling form of Sheba came flying through.

Mrs Crowley gave an uncharacteristic squeal as Sheba landed in front of her. Letting go of the generator, she aimed a kick at the wolfgirl's head. Sheba dodged out of the way, growling, and sank her teeth into the woman's ankle.

'You vicious little animal!' Mrs Crowley

screamed. She reached down and grabbed Sheba by the hair, hauling her head up. Sheba shook her head, trying to free herself, almost too frenzied to notice the glinting thing that had appeared in Mrs Crowley's hand. The woman had pulled Moon's knife from the professor's arm and was swinging it down towards her throat.

Sheba tried to move away, but her hair was held tight. The knife drew closer, cutting through the smoke in slow motion, now inches from her neck. Sheba saw the triumphant glint in Mrs Crowley's eyes; a look that rapidly changed to horror as something small and gruesome bounced off the nearest wall and onto her head.

Pyewacket!

Mrs Crowley screamed as the grubby imp perched on her shoulders, clawing and scrabbling at her face – just as the floor gave a violent lurch.

Sheba looked down. The floorboards had given way, opening up a fire-filled hole to the level below. For one horrible moment Sheba teetered, about to spill down into the flames, taking Pyewacket and Mrs Crowley with her – and then she found her balance.

She forced the wolf back down, deep inside, and stood up tall, wrapping both arms around Pyewacket.

With the last of her strength, she heaved him free of Mrs Crowley and, as he came, kicking and scratching, Sheba saw Mrs Crowley lose her footing and topple near the hole's edge.

For a second, a heartbeat, Sheba thought about reaching out and trying to grab her. But then Sister Moon's hand was on her shoulder, dragging her to safety . . . just as a burst of flames roared up from the hole, blocking Mrs Crowley from sight.

'We have to run!' Moon shouted.

And so they dashed across the floor, dodging fire and falling bricks, until they were back at the far door. Mama Rat and Gigantus were waiting for them, coughing and spluttering.

'She fell,' Sheba croaked. 'I couldn't stop her . . .'

But the others didn't care about that. Only that she was safe. They crowded round her, clapping her on the back, wrapping their arms about each other, filled with joy that they were all together again.

'Till! The mudlarks!' Sheba shouted, breaking free of the huddle. 'We still have to get them out!'

They turned to run back to the operating theatre, rushing to free the children before the fire took hold. Sheba followed, but not before sparing a backwards glance through the smoke to where the hazy silhouette of the professor stood, and before him the empty hole through which Mrs Crowley had vanished.

*

Later, as they herded the gaggle of dazed mudlarks out of the burning building, Till turned to Sheba and gave her a fierce, tight hug. The other children were just as grateful. They thronged the carnival troupe in a tearful huddle, unable to believe their long ordeal was finally over.

Sheba felt like collapsing onto the ground and gulping in mouthfuls of the clear night air, but she knew they couldn't stand around for long. It was only a matter of time before the police, already out in their hundreds, came to investigate the explosion.

'We have to go,' she said, her voice croaky with smoke. The others nodded and, keeping to the shadows, the group headed out of the hospital grounds, passing the crumpled form of the Major as they went.

Part of Sheba wanted to stay and tell the police what had happened. They might be in time to rescue the professor and the generator. They might be able to find the body of Mrs Crowley. Save her, even, if she wasn't already burnt to a crisp.

But it was more likely the police would laugh in their faces, all the way to the nearest cells. They were nothing but a gaggle of ragtag sideshow acts, after all. At the very worst, the police might even think they had stolen the generator themselves. Judging by all the soldiers, the Exhibition attack was being treated as a matter of national security, and Sheba didn't really fancy her head being stuck on a spike on top of Temple Bar.[xxxiv]

No, it was better that nobody knew they were involved. They had stopped Mrs Crowley and saved the children. That was all that mattered. As the first policemen came running, blowing their whistles and shouting for help, Sheba and the others slipped through the crowds on Hyde Park Corner and home to Brick Lane, with Till clutching Sheba's hand all the way.

CHAPTER NINETEEN

In which Sheba finds her home.

The morning edition of *The Times* was full of reports about the events in Hyde Park. The front page showed a drawing of the Crystal Palace with flames rising from a gaping hole in its side, and beneath it the article read:

BURGLARY AND BOMBS AT THE GREAT EXHIBITION

At around midnight last night, Hyde Park was host to a tragic spectacle. The Crystal Palace, site of the Great Exhibition of the Industry of All Nations, fell victim to a malicious and cowardly attack.

Persons unknown managed to gain access to the North Gallery by cutting through the glass wall. They then removed at least one of the exhibits, before placing an explosive device in the Refreshment Court. Thanks to the bravery of London's Fire Brigades, none of the other displays was damaged.

Prince Albert himself is due to inspect the damage this morning, and it is expected the Exhibition will remain closed for at least two days.

There was also a piece on the theft, which Sheba read eagerly:

FAILED ATTEMPT TO STEAL MR FARADAY'S GENERATOR

It seems that the target of last night's raid on the Great Exhibition was the electromagnetic impulse generator designed and built by Mr Michael Faraday, one of the Exhibition judges.

A revolutionary new design, the generator is capable of creating the strongest electrical impulses yet achieved, with its inventor claiming that one day similar machines will replace steam and water power throughout the nation.

Ultimately, however, the plot was foiled. The criminals chose one of the derelict buildings of the old St George's Hospital as their lair, which then caught fire. The first policemen on the scene discovered the missing device, and also apprehended two criminals. One was a Professor Euan Crowley of Rotherhithe, the other a Major Kapoor, recently discharged from the East India Company's Ramgarh Light Infantry.

Both men were severely injured and are now in police custody, while the generator has been returned to Mr Faraday.

Sheba folded the paper and placed it back on the kitchen table. No mention of Mrs Crowley, she realised. Had she been burnt to ashes in the blaze? Or had she somehow survived and escaped?

Perhaps it was best if they never found out. At least that way, Sheba wouldn't have to see her again.

It should have been us in the papers, though, she thought. Instead nobody would ever know who had really saved the day.

Although that wasn't quite true. The parlour at Brick Lane was full of little sleeping people who would remember. They filled up most of the floor space, curled around each other, gently snoring. And after all, everything they had done wasn't really about foiling burglaries or catching criminals. It had been a mission to keep those children safe.

Sheba hopped down from the table and started to stoke up the stove, ready to put some coffee on for breakfast.

*

A few hours later, everyone was sitting in the parlour, talking about the events of the night before. Upstairs in the bedroom, Gigantus had hauled up the tin bath and filled it with water from the street pump, which he'd warmed over the fire. The mudlarks were taking it in turns to have the first bath of their lives, and the sounds of whoops and splashes drifted down through the ceiling.

'But what happened when the bomb went off?'

Sheba was asking. 'How come you weren't hurt?'

'Luck, I suppose,' said Mama Rat. 'We all happened to be elsewhere. If we hadn't split up to find that woman, it might have been a different story.'

'And how did you get out without being caught? The place was crawling with soldiers when I left.'

'We all ran back to the east wing when we heard the blast,' said Gigantus. He was writing in his notebook again, pen scratching across the paper, just as if the events of the past few days had never happened. 'The guards were so busy with the fire, we managed to slip out of Sister Moon's hole in the glass and join the crowds.'

'And then we found this,' said Sister Moon. She held up the chipped marble that Till had given her. 'It must have fallen from your pocket. Before that, we thought you were stuck in the Palace, or you'd been hurt by the bomb. Then Pyewacket spotted you running down Rotten Row.'

'That was very clever of you, Pye,' said Sheba, as he puffed out his chest.

'I know,' he said, beaming.

'We saw you following Mrs Crowley into that old

hospital,' said Mama Rat. 'We would have caught up to you sooner, had it not been so crowded. Thank goodness we got there in time. What you did was very brave, Sheba.'

Sheba blushed beneath her fur. She didn't know what to say. She was saved from further embarrassment by the mudlarks coming down the stairs. It was strange to see them so clean and happy; they were like a completely different group of children. Sheba could see their faces properly now, without the coating of mud. There were rosy cheeks, freckles and happy smiles. They looked more like a school class on an outing than a bunch of kidnap victims, recently saved from certain death.

'I'll put some soup on,' said Mama Rat. 'Feed you lot up a bit. Won't be long until Large 'Arry reads my secret message, if Bartholomew rat gets his skates on.'

Soon after that, there was a knock at the door. Sister Moon opened it to reveal a group of nervous-looking figures, clad in shapeless, muddy rags, all trying to peep past her at the same time.

Sheba recognised Till's mother and father, along with another boy who might have been Barney Bilge (it was difficult to tell, because last time she saw him he had been completely covered in wet mud). Behind them were even more people, all clutching their caps in their hands and chattering excitedly.

When Moon stepped aside, they rushed through and gathered the children in such tight embraces that Sheba worried their stick-thin limbs might snap. The parlour was full to bursting, and the carnival acts found themselves pushed back against the stairs. But it was a heartwarming sight, and Sheba felt a lump in her throat, especially now she knew such a reunion would never be hers.

Her father was dead, her mother lost and her family fortune stolen by Mrs Crowley. She had nothing left. Not even the hope-filled daydreams of a normal life. It was like everything she had ever wanted had just been dangled before her eyes, only to be snatched away again. For ever.

She glanced up to see Gigantus blinking rapidly and pretending to look at something on the ceiling. She silently offered him her hanky, then had to wring the sodden piece of cloth out after he gave it back.

'You chaps . . .' said Till's father, as soon as the

hugging and kissing was over. ''Ow can we ever fank you? We never fought we'd see our dear little 'uns again, and now 'ere they are, all washed and everyfing! I never imagined a child of mine would live to 'ave a proper barf.'

'You're welcome,' said Sheba, Pyewacket and Sister Moon together. Seeing the reunion made everything they'd been through seem worthwhile.

'We is so used to losing young 'uns to the river and the sickness and a 'undred other fings,' said the father mudlark. 'It's our way of life, and no one but us seems to care. We didn't expect you to, neither, but I'm very glad to say we was wrong.'

Sheba and her friends beamed. The other families left with their children, after shaking the troupe's hands in turn. Till's family hung back, and accepted Mama Rat's offer of tea. They stayed for most of the afternoon, listening as the story of the rescue was retold. As Sheba heard it, she was struck by how incredible it sounded, but the mudlarks never once questioned anything. They only stopped every now and then to wail in terror or sympathy, or to heap praises on everyone.

At the end of the tale, they all broke into applause and Till hugged Sheba tightly.

'What will you do now?' Sheba asked. She didn't like the thought of her new friend going back to a life of dangerous scavenging, even if there were no longer strange mechanical creatures lurking in the mud.

'Well, miss,' said the father mudlark, 'meself, the missus, Till and 'er brothers will be leaving the city.'

'Leaving?' Till and Sheba said together.

'Yes,' said Till's mother. 'I 'ave a cousin what works on a farm down in Kent. A place called Stanhope. She's always said there's room for us there. The children can work picking 'ops, and Tam and me can labour in the fields.'

'It'll be a better life for us all,' said the father.

Till looked at Sheba with tearful eyes. 'I won't ever see you again, will I?'

Sheba shook her head, too heartbroken to speak.

'I don't know about that,' said Mama Rat.

'Aye. We often go down that way in the summer, when the fairs are on,' added Gigantus.

'We can find a way to make Plumpscuttle go to Kent,' said Sister Moon. 'Mama Rat and Sheba can trick him into doing almost anything.'

'Kent's a good place for doing magic,' Pyewacket added. 'Lots of ley lines crossing. Places of power coming out of your ear'oles.'

'Promise you'll come see me,' Till said, squeezing Sheba's hands. 'Promise!'

'I will, I promise!' Sheba said, laughing. Next summer was a long way away, but it was better than nothing.

With that, the mudlarks prepared to leave. Before heading out of the door, they bowed and smiled at each of them, making Sheba feel as though she was some kind of royalty. As she watched them disappear down Brick Lane on the way back to the river, she held the chipped marble Till had given her, back when they had first met. She looked at it for a moment, squeezed it tight, then took it upstairs to place inside her ebony box.

Afterwards, she sat for a long time, running her fingers over the carved jasmine flowers. *This box must have come from India, too*, she realised. *It must have been my mother's.* She imagined herself as a tiny child, huddled in the hold of a clipper ship with her dying mother beside her. Did she take it then? Did she cling on to it, even as they dragged Mama's cold body away? Or perhaps a kind member of the crew took pity on her and made sure she had it when they handed her over to the orphanage.

It made her think of Mrs Crowley's story again, opening everything up like a fresh wound. Those delicate, star-shaped flowers, just like the ones at the exhibition. But she had seen them somewhere else recently, too. Where had it been?

Shortly after that, they received another visitor: a messenger from the London Hospital. He brought them a note that said Plumpscuttle had almost fully recovered and would be returning the next day.

They all groaned. Without the horrible Plumpscuttle, their little house was quite a pleasant place to live. Now they would have to return to being slaves and exhibits.

'We should have charged those mudlarks for our services. Then we could have done a runner while misery-guts was on his sickbed,' said Pyewacket, as he crawled off to his cage to sulk.

'And what would they have paid us with, exactly?'

said Gigantus. 'Half a ton of raw sewage?'

'I'd rather have a load of rotten poo than that bully, any day,' Pyewacket called back from the yard.

Sheba was inclined to agree. Still, a free afternoon gave her time to run a small errand or two.

Leaving the others to repair things as much as possible, she padded upstairs to fetch an item hidden under a certain strongman's bed. While he was still scribbling in his journal, she slipped out of the house.

*

After making a brief stop-off in Whitechapel, Sheba caught an omnibus south of the river. She sat in the furthest corner, squashed against the side by a plump businessman in a stovepipe hat. Her hood was pulled low over her face, and she clutched the pennies she had borrowed from Mama Rat in her fist, waiting for the conductor. She was terrified she might miss her stop and end up lost in London, but there wasn't time to walk to her destination and back.

When the omnibus finally pulled up at a riverside tavern called the Angel, Sheba was glad to escape its cramped, sweaty confines and stretch her legs. She took a moment to look out at the river, safe now – at least from Major Kapoor and his machine – thanks to her and her friends. Although none of the hundreds of people working, steaming and sailing up and down the Thames knew a thing about it.

She could have stood there all day, working up the courage for what she had to do. Instead she forced her feet to walk along the Rotherhithe Wall and turn down Love Lane. After all, this was nothing compared to the scrapes and battles she had just faced.

A little further on, and she emerged on Paradise Street. A few doors down on her left was number 17.

Just as before, she slipped around the back and picked the lock with her hairpins. Just as before, her breath came quick and shallow, as she imagined Mrs Crowley sitting inside, waiting for her. *But she was burnt to ashes in the fire*, Sheba told herself. *Wasn't she?*

The house was silent and still again, although this time shards of daylight slipped in through the grimy windows, filling the air with glowing motes of dust.

Sheba tiptoed through the kitchen and up the stairs, all the while clutching the pistol in her coat pocket, just in case.

When she reached the third floor, she paused. There was the keyhole she had spied through. There was the room they had hidden in and there, on the dirty floorboards, was a rusty puddle of dried blood where Matthew had met his end.

Sheba had been thinking a lot about this place. She had been thinking especially of the paintings in that room, of the carved wood that framed them.

She took a deep breath and walked to the door, pushing it wide, then stepped into the room, pistol raised.

The high-backed armchair was there, a dark shape in the middle. Sheba squeezed the trigger, shooting a dart.

There was a soft *pop* of bursting leather as it hit the back of the empty chair.

But it was just a shadow.

Breathing a sigh of relief, Sheba looked around the room. Someone had been here, and they had left in a hurry. The furniture was toppled and strewn;

everything of value had been taken. Had it happened before they stole the generator or after? There was no way of telling.

But at least the paintings were still there.

Sheba moved closer, looking at the frames first. They were made of dark ebony and all around them were twining jasmine flowers. Just like the ones on her box.

Now that she knew, she took her time stepping backwards and looking up. She was finally going to meet her parents.

Her father first: a stern, proud-looking man. He wore the red uniform of the East India Company, his chest covered with medals. The dusty hills behind him must be somewhere in India. Maybe the place Sheba grew up. She tried to imagine him ordering her to be locked away, as Mrs Crowley had described. But he didn't look mean enough. And for him to die alone in a hospital bed, thousands of miles away . . .

It was too painful to think about. Instead, she turned to her mother. She was beautiful. She wore a dress of white silk and gazed out of the picture with a kind, loving face. And her eyes. They were the same shape, the same amber colour as hers. She recognised her now. The woman by the fountain, beckoning as Sheba ran to her.

Sheba stared at the painting, wanting to take in every detail before she left. She memorised her mother's hair, the shape of her nose, her lips. She peered closer, a breath stuck in her throat. Her hands . . . were the nails slightly pointed? Almost clawlike?

Sheba clutched her own hands together, squeezing hard. Could her mother have been like her? Half woman, half wolf? And if so, would she really have been ashamed of her daughter, like Mrs Crowley said? Deep in her bones, Sheba knew it wasn't true. After all, this woman in the painting had taken Sheba with her when she left India. She must have loved her fiercely to do that. Tears trickled down Sheba's face – she *was* someone's daughter. She *had* been loved. This changed everything.

Sheba wished she could pack up the portraits and take them with her – she wanted to gaze at them for hours – but they were too big, and would involve too much explaining. For now, this was her secret. She would leave them here in this dusty house, knowing she could slip back whenever she wished to gaze at them again. It was time to go now. There would be many hours to think about her parents and what might have happened to them.

*

Later on, at suppertime, they all gathered around the kitchen table for their last free meal without Plumpscuttle. Out in the yard, Raggety and Flossy had an extra helping of oats, and Sheba ladled out penny dip into bowls as Sister Moon handed them around.

Mama Rat was beaming. The other rats had brought her a present that morning: a little baby ratling they had found abandoned in a sewer somewhere. She was feeding it scraps of chewed meat from her own mouth.

'I'm going to call you Paul,' she cooed, as the scraggly thing let out a squeak.

Sheba concentrated on keeping down her mutton.

Pyewacket was feeling jolly too. He was telling

everyone about his heroics of the other night in great detail, carefully missing out the parts where he had nearly wet himself with terror.

The only person who wasn't in a good mood was Gigantus. He was obviously having trouble with his writing, and kept scribbling out passages in his journal in between mouthfuls. Sheba thought she knew what would cheer him up, though.

When the stew was finished, she stood on her stool and cleared her throat, nervously.

'If you please,' she said, 'I have an announcement to make.'

All eyes turned to her.

'Today I took the book Gigantus has been writing—'

'You did *what*?!' The big man jumped from his stool, his face going pink with rage.

Sheba pressed on. 'I took your book and showed it to the printers on Whitechapel Road,' she said. 'I'm really sorry, but when I found it – by accident, of course – I just couldn't stop reading it. It deserves better than being hidden under your mattress, Gigantus. And the printers thought so too. They read it there and then, and they want to publish it in their magazine.'

'My book?' said Gigantus. 'In a real magazine?'

He stood silent, steely eyes fixed on Sheba, beneath a craggy frown. She began to wonder if she might have done something really stupid, when Gigantus suddenly rushed around the table at her. She screwed her eyes shut and flinched, but instead of pounding her into paste, he grabbed her in a gentle bear hug.

'Thank you,' he said, tears in his eyes. 'I should be furious with you, but thank you. *Thank you.*'

'Are you going to publish it under your own name?' Sheba asked, when the big man had finally let go.

'I don't think Gabriel Greepthick would go down too well,' he said. 'Gertrude Lacygusset is much better.'

'Gabriel!' Pyewacket screamed with laughter.

'Well, it's better than Jack Parpfettle,' said Gigantus.

Pyewacket's fanged mouth dropped wide open. 'How did you . . . ? Who told you . . . ?'

Gigantus just winked and tapped his crooked nose with a finger.

'I don't actually know any of your real names,' said Sheba. It was something she'd never even thought about.

'Zhā Lā,' said Sister Moon, tipping her new top hat. 'But if it's easier, you can call me Zara.'

'And I'm Marie,' said Mama Rat. 'And how about you, dearie? Do you know your real name?'

'It's Sheba,' she said. 'I know that now for sure. Sheba is the name my mother gave me.'

'Well, now we've all been properly introduced, I think it's high time for a celebration,' said Mama Rat. The rest of the carnival cheered.

At least until they heard the front door slam.

Plumpscuttle's furious voice echoed from the parlour.

'What in the name of Prince Albert's moustache has happened to my pigging front door? And why does my house stink like a week-old chamber pot? Has someone been carving chunks out of my wall? And the bath is out! Who said you lot could have a bath? Get in here and explain yourselves!'

*

Plumpscuttle's stay in hospital had done nothing to improve his temper. His face was still puffy and bruised, and thick bandages could be seen beneath his shirt. The thing that seemed to have annoyed him most, however, was paying for the privilege of having his life saved.

He spent the best part of an hour shouting before stamping up the stairs to his bedroom. Then he noticed the blanket covering the smashed window, and came back down to holler at them all over again. Finally he left them to get ready for a show, 'to pay for all the damage to the pigging house'.

For once they all joined Pyewacket in making rude gestures behind his back. Then they set about putting up the sheets and tarpaulins for showtime.

When Plumpscuttle's dozy nephew turned up to man the door, they were just hanging up the last string of lanterns. Phineas stood watching them, while he rooted around in his left nostril with a pudgy finger.

Right on cue, Plumpscuttle emerged from his room dressed in an almost-clean suit. He was verging on cheerful, clearly glad at being out of the hospital ward. 'Right, come on, you lot – it's SHOWTIME!' he announced.

With a last check that their costumes were correct, the acts darted off to their various parts of the house, ready for the show to begin.

Sheba smoothed out her cloak as she sat on her little stool in the corner of their bedroom. She stared glumly at the sheets hanging in front of her, watching as the silhouette of Sister Moon practised a few lightning-quick dashes across the room, and listening to the sounds of the others going through their acts. A few hours ago, she had been fighting villains and rescuing lost children, and now she was sitting like a sack of potatoes, waiting for people to shriek at the sight of her.

As the first customers came thumping up the stairs, she tried to make herself look as wolfish as possible. It was hard. Once you had spent a few days fighting hand to hand with twisted machines and murderous villains, sitting in a sideshow seemed impossibly dull. *I'm so much more than just a lonely half-wolf now*, she thought. *I'm part of a team. And I have a mother that loves me. Or at least I did.*

And that very team – those brave adventurers, those bickering oddments; those wonderful, unique, hilarious, quarrelsome misfits – were her family now.As much as . . . no, *more than* . . . her lost, unknown parents ever were or could be.

Instead of forcing herself to look freakish, she sat up tall. She flexed her claw-tipped fingers and shook out her hair. She held up her chin, gritted her sharp little teeth and stared out at the audience with flashing, amber eyes.

This is who I am, she said to herself. *I don't need to hide behind the wolf. Let them see my furry skin, my pointed nails. Let them snigger and say cruel things about me. I don't care what they think. I am proud. I am me.*

Sheba picked up her comb, running it through her chestnut-brown curls, taking out the tangles. She looked out over the rooftops of London and smiled.

Everyone always said she had a lovely head of hair.

NOTES

i. The stone walkways beside the Thames, known as the Embankment, weren't built until 1862. Before then, warehouses and buildings spilled down to the river's edge all over the place. There were sets of stairs for getting down to the river at low tide, pontoons and jetties everywhere and, of course, plenty of sewage pipes gushing with all sorts of disgusting liquid.

ii. The original Fiji Mermaid was an exhibit in the museum of P. T. Barnum in 1842. Although it was *obviously* the top half of a stuffed monkey sewn onto the tail of a fish, many people believed it was actually real. And not one of them thought to ask about underwater bananas.

iii. A yard is equal to three feet, which is about ninety centimetres.

iv. The Exhibition was planned and organised by Prince Albert, the husband of Queen Victoria. Countries from around the world were invited to display their greatest technology, but most of the space was reserved for Britain, so it was really just a chance for the Empire to do a bit of showing off. It was very popular though, with over six million visitors. Public toilets had to be invented especially for it, and it cost one penny to go (which is why some people say they are going to 'spend a penny' when they're off for a wee).

v. £12 doesn't sound like very much but, in today's money, it was worth about £900. Or the price of two cows, if you prefer currency that moos.

vi. In the 1640s, Matthew Hopkins called himself the 'Witchfinder General' and went about the country accusing innocent men and women of being witches. In just two short years he had three hundred people executed and earned himself a terrifying reputation.

Pyewacket, *Vinegar Tom* and *Grizzel Greedigut* were imps that he claimed belonged to one of the first witches he caught. Which shows that, as well as being disgustingly evil, he was quite good at making up names. He might have made a good children's author.

vii. The Victorian London skyline would have been completely different from that of today. The current Houses of Parliament were still being built, meaning there was no Clock Tower (or 'Big Ben') and the tallest building in the city would have been St Paul's. Or 'The Onion', as it probably would have been nicknamed today.

viii. 'Dust heaps' were the Victorian version of recycling. Towering piles of London's rubbish were stacked in teetering mounds, while their owners paid workers to sift through it all, sorting out anything they could sell. You could actually make a lot of money doing this. A dust heap owner in the time of Charles Dickens was worth £111,000 when he died (which is about £8 million today).

ix. Ballad singers had been walking London's streets for hundreds of years, singing popular songs and selling sheets of music. If you heard a tune you liked, you could stop one and buy a copy, then rush home and bash it out on your pianoforte. Or just sit and stare at the notes, which didn't have quite the same effect.

x. These were known as Bowie knives, named after a famous knife fighter called Jim Bowie. In Mississippi in 1827, he was in a big fight, when he pulled out an eight-inch hunting blade with a clip point and a cross guard. Everyone was very impressed, although it didn't stop him being shot, stabbed, shot again and then stabbed once more for luck.

xi. Although, if someone had used a microscope, they would have seen that there were *plenty* of cholera bacteria living there. In fact, they were having a lovely time.

xii. They were gritty because Victorian bakers in the poorer parts of London used to mix all sorts of things into their flour to save money. Plaster and chalk were favourites, as was alum, which was seriously poisonous. Deadly dumplings, they should have been called.

xiii. 'Peelers' was a slang word for the police. The name came from Prime Minister Robert Peel, who founded the Metropolitan Police in 1829, Britain's first police force. This was also why they were called 'bobbies'. Other Victorian names for the police were 'crushers', 'bluebottles' and 'mutton-shunters'. And there were probably a few more that are far too rude to print.

xiv. Death and mourning were very much a part of Victorian life. Probably because you were likely to die of something nasty, especially if you were a child. There were lots of strange traditions involved with mourning. These included taking photographs alongside the dead body, making jewellery from bits of the person's hair and covering all the mirrors in the house to stop their soul getting trapped inside. Mourners also wore black for a long time after a loved one died. Queen Victoria stayed in her mourning dress for the rest of her life after she lost Prince Albert. (Hopefully she remembered to wash it now and then.)

xv. It was fashionable for Victorian men to grow the whiskers on their cheeks as long as they could, while shaving the rest of their face. Also known as 'mutton chops', this style was only beaten in the 'stupid facial hair' stakes by the 'doorknocker', which was a U-shaped strip of beard starting from the sides of the mouth and meeting up under the chin.

xvi. The East India Company began in 1600, as a group of British merchants. By 1850 it had crushed and conquered most of India, Southeast Asia and Hong Kong, and had a private army twice the size of the Queen's. They stole land, traded in slaves and caused disasters such as the Great Bengal Famine of 1770, in which ten million people died. It's no wonder you'd want to run away from them, really.

xvii. Although he would never admit it, Mr Wobble

was Pyewacket's imaginary friend for most of his childhood. It is very hard to draw pictures when you have enormous fingers and the arms of an orangutan, so Mr Wobble looked like a big caramel pudding, with a smaller caramel pudding for a head. Hence the name.

xviii. People think that the Thames is the only river in London, but there are actually many smaller tributaries that once flowed into it and now run underground. As well as the Neckinger, these include the Effra, the Tyburn, the Falconbrook, the Rom and the Fleet – which once ran all the way down from Hampstead Heath and gave its name to Fleet Street.

xix. HMS *Swiftsure* was a British warship that was used in the Napoleonic wars. After fighting in the Battle of the Nile, she was captured by the French and fought against her builders at the Battle of Trafalgar. She was then brought home and ended her days as a prison ship: a floating hulk used to keep hundreds of jailed criminals in because it was much cheaper than building an actual prison. Spindlecrank must have rescued her from this sad fate, although she would have had to spend a very long time scrubbing all the stains out.

xx. The Highway was a dark and dangerous part of London, made infamous by the 'Ratcliff Highway Murders' of 1811. Two families were attacked in their homes, and the story was made famous by newspapers all across the country. Victorians loved reading about other people getting horribly murdered. It probably made them feel a bit better about how short, painful and brutal their own lives were.

xxi. This was just about the rudest thing you could shout at a Victorian lady.

xxii. Michael Faraday was a scientist, famous for studying electricity and electromagnets. His discoveries helped make electricity usable as an energy source, and he was also involved with planning and judging the Great Exhibition.

xxiii. Anne Boleyn had the bad luck of being Henry VIII's second wife. He grew bored of her after a few years and, instead of getting a divorce, thought it would be much easier just to have her head chopped off. Well, easier for him, at least.

xxiv. Jane Grey was Queen of England for nine whole days, following the death of Edward VI. Edward's sister Mary wasn't very happy about it, and had Jane's head cut off so she could become queen herself. Head-lopping was pretty much a national sport in those days.

xxv. White phosphorus is a chemical that was used to make matches. The poor workers in match factories often suffered from 'phossy jaw': fumes from all the white phosphorus they used made their jawbones rot away, leading to horrible injuries and often death. And yet it took sixty years to be banned, becoming illegal in 1910.

xxvi. This was a device made of two rollers that you could feed laundry through, to squeeze all the water out. And it was something you wanted to avoid getting any dangly parts of your body trapped in, at all costs.

xxvii. The original site of the Crystal Palace was in Hyde Park, but it was moved to south London in 1854.

xxviii. Newer London houses had toilets that flushed with water (straight into the Thames) but old ones still had outdoor toilets, with a pit beneath that was emptied, every now and then, by 'night soil men'. Probably the worst job in the whole of the city, and that was saying something.

xxix. This track through Hyde Park was created by King William III, and was originally called 'Route de roi' (French for 'King's Road'). If you were a fashionable Londoner in the eighteenth century, you would walk up and down it in your finest clothes every weekend, looking smug. Bonus fact: it was the first piece of road ever to have artificial lighting, because the park was riddled with highwaymen.

xxx. Visitors to the Exhibition were very disappointed at the diamond, as it hadn't been cut very well and didn't sparkle. It was re-cut in 1852 and added to the Crown Jewels.

xxxi. A shuttered lantern had little doors (or shutters) you could close to dim the amount of light. They were also known as 'dark lanterns'.'

xxxii. Sexism was *incredibly* bad in Victorian times. As well as not being allowed to vote, as an educated woman, pretty much your only option for employment was to become the private teacher to the children of a rich family. You also had to wear ridiculous skirts and corsets and spend a *lot* of time doing watercolours or embroidery.

xxxiii. Nineteenth-century surgery involved no anaesthetic and no antiseptic, which made it very painful, very risky and quite probably fatal.

xxxiv. Temple Bar Gate was an elaborate stone gateway that once stood at the entrance to the City of London. As well as London Bridge and the Tower, it was a place your head might end up, once it had been chopped off for treason.

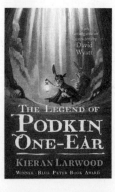

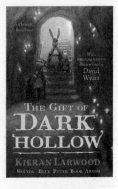

Journey to the fantastical world
of the Five Realms!

**Winner of the Best Story Blue
Peter Book Award**

*A thick white blanket covers the wide slopes of the
band of hills known as the Razorback Downs . . .*

Podkin is the son of a warrior chieftain. He knows
that one day it will be up to him to lead his warren
and guard it in times of danger. But for now, he's
quite happy to laze around annoying his older
sister, Paz, and playing with his baby brother,
Pook. Then Podkin's home is brutally attacked,
and the young rabbits are forced to flee. The
terrifying Gorm are on the rampage, and no one
and nowhere is safe. With danger all around
them, Podkin must protect his family, uncover his
destiny, and attempt to defeat the most horrifying
enemy rabbitkind has ever known.

Discover Fantastic Faber Reads